There is a moment when the reality of the individual – the personal assumptions, illusions and delusions through which he views others, the little games of pride and malice with which he protects himself – must confront the greater reality of the world. It is in that moment that things both end and begin.

In this sharp and original collection of stories Carl Djerassi takes that moment and uses it to illuminate our lives. Shrewd and ironic, he shows himself to be a compassionate observer of the human condition – a skilful writer whose understanding of the absurdities of individual triumphs and disasters helps us to better understand ourselves.

'Brilliant, elegant stories, sparkling with wit and word-play, exploring human nature, the nature of literature, and the nature of *thought*. Cleverness at its human best. The tales are all remarkable individuals.' Iris Murdoch

CARL DJERASSI

THE FUTURIST and Other Stories

Macdonald

A Macdonald Book

Copyright © Carl Djerassi 1988

First published in Great Britain in 1988 by
Futura Publications, a Division of
Macdonald & Co (Publishers) Ltd
London & Sydney

This Macdonald edition published in 1989

Acknowledgments:
'Castor's Dilemma' first appeared in the *Hudson Review*;
'Maskenfreiheit' in the *Crescent Review*; 'What's Tatiana
Troyanos Doing in Spartacus's Tent?' in *Exquisite Corpse*; and
'The Toyota Cantos' in *Frank: An International Journal of
Contemporary Writing and Art*.

*All characters in this publication are fictitious
and any resemblance to real persons, living or dead,
is purely coincidental.*

All rights reserved.
No part of this publication may be reproduced,
stored in a retrieval system, or transmitted, in any
form or by any means without the prior
permission in writing of the publisher, nor be
otherwise circulated in any form of binding or
cover other than that in which it is published and
without a similar condition including this
condition being imposed on the subsequent
purchaser.

British Library Cataloguing in Publication Data
Djerassi, Carl, *1923*–
  The futurist and other stories.
  I. Title
  813'.54[F]
  ISBN 0 356 17500 6

Reproduced, printed and bound in Great Britain by
Hazell Watson & Viney Limited
Member of BPCC plc
Aylesbury, Bucks, England

Macdonald & Co (Publishers) Ltd
Greater London House
Hampstead Road
London NW1 7QX
A member of Maxwell Pergamon Publishing Corporation plc

Contents

The Futurist	7
Noblesse Oblige	17
The Dacriologist	29
Castor's Dilemma	47
The Glyndebourne Heist	67
The Psomophile	83
Sleight-Of-Mind	95
Maskenfreiheit	103
First-Class Nun	123
What's Tatiana Troyanos Doing In Spartacus's Tent?	139
The Toyota Cantos	145

For
Diane Middlebrook

The Futurist

'Two twenty-five. Two fifty. Two seventy-five, thank you. Three hundred. Three twenty. Three twenty ...' The auctioneer slowed down. The 1912 Boccioni was a powerful painting and a large one at that – at least four feet by seven. But 320,000 pounds sterling? thought Donna Massingham. It had taken less than a minute to reach this world record for an Italian Futurist, at which point only three bidders remained. One, spectacularly invisible, was a telephone caller, communicating with the auctioneer via a prim young woman on the podium, phone in hand. Another was in one of the front rows; Donna couldn't make him out, she was too far back, but she could see his paddle popping up from time to time. This seemed like bad manners compared to those of the third competitor. He seemed to be sitting somewhere nearby – she could see the auctioneer's eyes hover in her neighbourhood each time the bid was raised. He must be one of those mystery buyers, Donna thought, who tweaks his left ear lobe or scratches his right nostril – each tweak or scratch worth an education at Harvard.

She should know what that cost, having majored in art history there, before graduate school at Penn and her present assistant curatorship at the museum. Her responsibility did not cover museum acquisitions, but she loved to attend auctions in her speciality – early twentieth-century European art. She'd been to Sotheby's and Christie's many times, but always in New York. Now she was attending her first London auction and admiring the low-key, Oxbridge manner in which the man on the podium – really one's image of a banker – conducted the affair. The last 'three twenty' had been accompanied by a nod in the direction of the woman holding the telephone, indicating that the top bid was currently somewhere abroad. The auctioneer peered over his glasses at the front row, but no hand was waved this time. His lips had parted to announce for the third and final time the winning bid, when just the faintest suspicion of a smile appeared on his face. Before the exultant 'three forty' had registered on the audience, the woman on the phone was whispering. She hung up as the auctioneer glanced at her. The Boccioni had been sold for 340,000 pounds, not counting the 10 per cent sales commission.

'Boy, isn't that something? Half a million dollars for this Boccioni,' Donna said aloud, to nobody in particular.

The man on her right, whom she had not noticed before, turned to her. 'Don't you like this painting?'

'It's magnificent,' said Donna, 'But look at the pre-sale estimate.' She pointed to the open catalogue in her lap. 'That's three times what they listed here.'

'It happens all the time,' retorted the man, 'when two collectors want the same lot and can afford it. But this is a rare one; the woman's head could've been painted by one of the Paris cubists. It really ought to hang next to Picasso's portrait of Ambroise Vollard. But it won't.' He chuckled.

'Do you know who got the Boccioni?' asked Donna.

'Yes,' he replied slyly. 'I even know the wall on which it will hang after it's been reframed.' It was the beginning of a conversation that eventually led Donna's neighbour to invite her for a visit to his private art collection near Milano when he learned that she was heading for an art vacation in Italy.

Donna's eyes were adjusting from the Italian sunshine to the subdued light coming through the French windows. Direct sunlight was never permitted to shine into the high-ceilinged room where they were sitting on an eighteenth-century sofa. Two matching upholstered chairs and two side tables, covered with stacks of gallery announcements, art magazines and auction catalogues, completed the sparse furnishings. Sparse, that is, if one didn't count the paintings on the walls, or the plexiglass cubes scattered throughout the room on which some sculptures seemed to be floating.

When August Himmelschwanz said, 'Call me Gus,' Donna had been placed in a special class – the Americans whom Himmelschwanz wanted to impress. At home, in Düsseldorf, he was usually *Herr Generaldirektor*; on his estate in Northern Italy, which housed his collection of Italian Futurists, he was 'Augusto' to his carefully selected circle of Italian admirers. To occasional British visitors, like Sir Hugh Eckersley, who had written *the* major English text on the Futurists, he was simply 'Himmelschwanz'. It sounded like a curse when bellowed by Sir Hugh in his *basso profundo*.

The moment Himmelschwanz had learned at the London auction that Donna was a museum curator – the 'assistant' in her official title might have cost her the invitation – and that Italy was part of her holiday itinerary, he suggested that she inspect his collection. Ten days later, she arrived in a rented Ford Fiesta, and now he was 'Gus' and she 'Donna'.

They'd been wandering in the gardens surrounding his seventeenth-century Italian villa, now known as Villa Cielo. Entering through the French windows, they had finally arrived in his favourite place: the first-floor drawing-room containing some of the fruits of what he called his 'didactic collecting'. This majestic room – perhaps forty-five or more feet long from entrance door to French windows, and some twenty feet wide – contained the gems of Himmelschwanz's collection of early Futurists. It was the room where the Boccioni would hang once it arrived from London and had passed through the hands of the Milano establishment that did all of Himmelschwanz's framing.

Shortly after he had acquired the mansion, Himmelschwanz had had all the electric fixtures ripped out. He was not interested in candelabra or other ornate lamps; only the most modern track lighting system with adjustable spotlights would do for his Villa Cielo. Cesare Villotti, the village electrician, had become almost a full-time employee of the Himmelschwanz establishment. He had been called many times to make alterations: install a dimmer; add another track; replace some of the spotlights; and help with the perpetual re-hanging of the pictures. Himmelschwanz insisted on himself making all decisions pertaining to the correct illumination of his collection, and on being present whenever a painting was hung or a sculpture positioned. Cesare Villotti was like a village doctor who had to respond at the oddest hours to any summons from the local manor house. Whenever

Himmelschwanz bought a new painting, or loaned one out to some museum (he insisted that the loan be identified only as *Privatsammlung*, his private signature for the cognoscenti), Villotti was summoned to help in the rearrangement of the wall space and lighting.

Cesare knew nothing about modern art, but he was proud of the Italian names that he read on the labels: Severini, Prampolini, Russolo. And in Himmelschwanz's presence, Cesare was deeply conscious of being Italian. In his early twenties, he had spent several years in Switzerland as a *Gastarbeiter*. He'd learned very early, and especially on lonely weekends, that this term was a euphemism for 'second-class foreigner'. He had never lost his sensitivity towards the disdain that many Swiss and Germans showed for foreign workers, especially the southern Europeans.

And he never let on that he understood German. Many times, Cesare would be standing on a ladder fiddling with the lights, while Himmelschwanz instructed some visitor as to why one could not really depend on the locals: they were charming, simple folk; they had a sense of humour; he loved their songs, but when it came to reliability ...

More than once Cesare had been tempted to climb down the ladder and walk out, with his middle finger stuck up in the classic Italian gesture. 'Take your *verdammte* bulb and screw it in yourself!' But he always resisted the temptation when he remembered what an enviable sinecure his Villa Cielo position really was.

Himmelschwanz gave the dimmer a half turn. The works were not arranged by artists' names, but grouped by style. The wall facing the sofa seemed to Donna designed to illustrate the similarity and divergence between the Paris Cubists and the Italian Futurists. There was another Boccioni of 1912, a Carlo Carra of the same year, a very early Prampolini, a Soffici with Cubist overtones. Among these, in the very middle of the long wall, hung two Cubist oils, by Picasso or Braque, which seemed virtual copies.

When Cesare Villotti had suggested to his employer that separate dimmers for two paintings hanging right next to each other, and furthermore nearly identical, was a waste of money, he received his first and only art lecture. It was precisely because they were so similar, yet painted by two of the giants of the early part of this century, that they had to be capable of being lit separately. Moreover, it amused Himmelschwanz to have his visitors guess which was the Picasso and which the Braque. By playing with the lights, he could focus their attention first on one and then the other.

'*Signore*',' Villotti had asked, 'could you have told them apart? I don't see any signatures.'

'They left them unsigned, deliberately. But all you'd have to do is look at the back.' It was not an invitation to lift them off the wall; it was simply a statement of fact.

'But you, *Signore*, now that you've had them for a while, can you tell which is which?'

Himmelschwanz had shrugged. 'If I stand close by and study them very carefully, yes. But I don't have to do this. The Picasso is always on the right. I never change these two.'

'Hm,' was Villotti's sole response. Later on, when he'd completed the final adjustment of the lights he lifted first one and then the other painting from their hooks to inspect the collage of museum labels on the back of each picture. 'Hm,' he said again, this time to himself.

*

'The cook and maid are both off today,' Himmelschwanz said. 'Why don't you look around while I make some coffee?'

Donna headed straight for the two oils in the centre of the room. For her they were like old friends; her graduate thesis had dealt with the Cubists. By the time her host had returned, she was in a corner inspecting a 1914 ink drawing by Giacomo Balla that she would never have recognized had it not been for the carefully printed label.

She accepted the proffered cup of coffee. 'It's simply breathtaking,' she said. 'Now I understand why you had to get that Boccioni in London.'

Himmelschwanz's look bordered on the ecstatic. Compliments by art professionals meant much more to him than the effusions, tinged with envy, that he received from fellow collectors.

'But tell me,' she continued, 'where did you get that Picasso on the left, next to the Severini?'

'Are you sure that's a Picasso?'

Donna caught the sly note in the question. 'I'd be willing to bet it is. I just looked at it.'

'Would you really?'

'What I mean is – I'm certain about the Picasso. But no, I wouldn't bet with you. First of all, how could I bet with my host about something when I knew ahead of time I'd win? Wouldn't that be ungracious?'

'Any other reason why you wouldn't bet?' he persisted.

'Well, we aren't in the same league when it comes to betting, are we, Gus?' Donna blushed when she realized that she had actually taken him up on his 'Call me Gus' invitation.

Himmelschwanz seemed too excited to notice. His eyes swept the room. 'Do you see that painted teapot over there, next to the wooden flowers?' He pointed to one of the plexiglass cubes in the room. 'Do you know whose they are?'

Donna had caught the patronizing implication of the question. She wished she could have put him in his place. 'No,' she conceded, 'I don't.'

'Which do you like better?'

'The teapot,' she said, 'It's really quite handsome. Who did it?'

'Balla. He did these in the twenties – painted wooden flowers, furniture, ceramics. Here, I'll bet you this teapot that the painting on the left,' he stressed the last word, 'is not by Picasso. You wanna bet?'

Donna smiled politely at the clumsy Americanism. 'But what could I bet in return?' She had no idea of the value of Balla's ceramic, except that almost anything of his was likely to cost at least a few thousand dollars. She got up from the sofa; Himmelschwanz had sounded so cocksure. But no – the Picasso was hanging on the left.

'Isn't the teapot good enough?' he asked. 'Or have you changed your mind?'

'If you mean about the Picasso, no. I haven't changed my mind. But I have nothing to offer in exchange for this Balla.'

'I know something that you can offer me – in the unlikely event that you lose.' My God, she thought, so that's it? And here we are out in the sticks, the servants gone.

But Himmelschwanz continued, 'I've decided that the time has come to prepare a complete catalogue of my collection and I'd prefer it to be in English. I've been looking around for somebody who'd undertake the job. How about it? If you lose the bet, you'll write the catalogue.'

Donna's face at that moment should have been painted by a Futurist – someone like Balla who had been infatuated by movement and change; as in his speeding car paintings, a masterful example of which was hanging in this room. Her initial fear had changed to relief, then surprise, and finally conviction.

'All right ...' she said, after a pause. 'Who's going to settle who won?'

'You will,' he said. 'Just lift the painting off the wall and look at the labels on the back. There must be at least half a dozen – including one from Christie's, where I bought it.' He leaned back in the sofa. 'Go on. Lift it off the hook,' he coaxed.

To Donna Massingham he looked the way one of her professors had during the final exam for her thesis, after having thrown her a tricky question. Seeing his learned smirk dissolve into politeness when he heard her answer, had been delicious.

In measured steps she reached the wall and removed the painting on the left. She did not allow herself a glow. She walked to the sofa, the painting hanging by its wire on her two middle fingers, and handed it, face up, to Himmelschwanz.

He didn't look at it or turn it over. He acted like a poker player holding a royal flush who didn't even ask to see his opponent's hand. 'The Braque can fool you,' he began, consolingly.

'Not really,' replied Donna. She lifted the lid of the Balla teapot and peered inside. 'It's never been used, has it?'

NOBLESSE OBLIGE

Sybil Stirling was in no mood for an examination, but there was sure to be one. Arturo was her first live-in lover, at least the first she'd mentioned to her parents. Should she have prepared Arturo? It had seemed better not to; he'd likely become defensive in an aggressive sort of way.

'*Mi amor,*' she'd started. She'd never learned how to roll the 'r', but she knew he liked to be caressed in Spanish by this very WASP daughter of a very WASP family. 'My parents are here for a bankers' convention. I got tickets for the theatre …'

'What to?' The interruption was typical of Arturo Flores. Even though he'd stopped working in the Public Defender's office, he still acted on occasion like a trial lawyer.

'*The House of Bernarda Alba.* I know you like Lorca. This is Tom Stoppard's version.'

The young man's smile lingered. 'Will your parents like it?'

Sybil shrugged. 'We'll see. But I know they're looking forward to meeting you. What do you think about St Honoré's for dinner? It used to be my father's favourite restaurant before they moved east. It's a stuffy place, but the food is first class.'

'And terribly overpriced,' Arturo had added.

'Don't worry, my father always picks up the tab. Remember? He's the president of the bank. But have you been to St Honoré's?'

'I was taken there once by someone trying to impress me.'

'And did he?' she asked coyly.

'No, she didn't,' was all he said.

Sybil Stirling had an extensive wardrobe, as befitted a young architect with a substantial income. A final inspection in her full-length mirror convinced Sybil that this was the correct choice for the mediating role she was going to play: no flashiness, just underplayed conservative elegance. It also seemed the right ensemble for St Honoré's, down to the Hermès scarf. As she left the bedroom, she wondered what Arturo would wear.

Her unconscious preference for an interview suit left her unprepared for what she found. In his champagne-coloured linen suit, white open-necked silk shirt and yellowish-tan silk ascot, he might have been cast in a movie as a young Latin lover.

'*Amor*, you look dashing …' she started, because it was true. He was a good inch shorter than Sybil, but she loved his taut body and springy gait, his aggressive self-confidence. The carefully trimmed black beard added a seductively demonic touch.

'But?' He moved toward her, with his boxer's step, his left hand gently cupping her chin.

'But nothing, Arturo. It's just …'

'…that this is not the right 'kohs-tyum' for St Honoré's?'

Her laugh was slightly forced. 'Never mind "*le costume*". What about "*la cravate*"?'

'*No te preocupas, muchacha*,' he replied and kissed her.

*

Mr and Mrs Alan B. Stirling, III, were sitting at a corner table facing the entrance. They'd been offered the most prominent spot in the dining-room: they looked exactly like the clientele to which St Honoré's wished to cater. Mrs Stirling wore a classic black Chanel suit – the real thing, bought at Bonwit-Teller – a single strand of pearls draped around her neck, and very little make-up. She must have been a striking woman in her youth and even now, as she approached sixty, there was nothing dowager-like about her tall, trim frame, her creamy skin, her light brown hair and the thick, straight eyebrows that gave her eyes an oriental look.

The *maître d'* was leaning solicitously over her husband's impeccably pin-striped shoulder; he was addressing him by name. Alan Stirling expected such recognition, yet he was pleased by it. But the banker's expression changed perceptibly when he caught sight of Sybil, his only daughter, towering – or so it seemed to him – over a miniature, bearded Rudolph Valentino, heading straight toward them. A waiter was trying to stop the young couple, but Arturo, with his arm on Sybil's elbow, almost tangoed her to the table before the waiter could intercept this especially flagrant violator of the restaurants' dress code.

'Mrs Stirling, I'm Arturo Flores.' Arturo had two ways of pronouncing his name: this time he chose the extra long roll of the 'r'. 'I've been looking forward to this dinner,' he said and kissed her hand. Moving past the stunned *maître d'*, he addressed her husband. 'It's very generous of you to join us at St Honoré's and the theatre. I hope you like Lorca.'

Both the waiter and the *maître d'* silently conceded defeat. Sybil was the only one to appreciate the strategy involved in getting around the two tie-policemen and the subtle irony in Arturo's behaviour toward her parents. Arturo was no lady's hand-kisser, nor was he usually deferential toward elder men, especially when he felt he was being subjected to Anglo scrutiny. He had a delicately balanced Chicano chip on his shoulder that neither four years at the University of California nor Yale Law School had removed. He never forgot that he was the only Flores in his immediate family who had ever attended college.

Sybil wanted no fencing match and was too independent to be seeking parental approval. She'd made up her mind long ago that Arturo Flores suited her in every respect. She knew that her mother respected her judgment and would support her in any choice pertaining to men. She was less certain about her father: each new beau had to be questioned, tested, and judged.

This time, there were two problems she'd never faced before. Arturo had moved in with her, not she with him. Was her father going to think that this man was sponging off a wealthy banker's daughter? The other was his name. Her father claimed not to be prejudiced, and he probably wasn't at his bank; the subject hardly ever rose to the top of the steep pyramid he commanded. But a potential 'Sybil Flores'?

Menu in hand, Stirling turned to Arturo. 'Will you have anything to drink before we order?' He turned to the waiter. 'I'll have a Campari with soda,' he added, 'and so will my wife.'

'Make it three,' interjected Sybil, hoping that Arturo would take the hint.

He didn't. 'Nothing right now, thanks.'

I'll give this point to Daddy, thought Sybil, for

whom this dinner had become something of a contest. He had made the bigger effort.

Although this was Arturo's second time at St Honoré's, he was again shocked by the prices on the menu. Christ, he thought, it's indecent to spend that much on a meal. I guess *el Papa* doesn't care.

The women made their choices and the waiter bowed toward the older man. Instead of ordering, Alan Stirling addressed Arturo. 'What are you having, Mr Flores?'

A nice gesture, not calling him Arturo, thought Sybil, and advanced the score 2-0 in her father's favour.

Arturo had studied the menu as sociological literature, rather than in preparation for a choice. The pompous descriptions of the various items amused him. As he looked up from his menu he realized that two pairs of eyes were studying him. The waiter, his pencil waggling over his pad, looked down his nose. Arturo didn't mind; he was sure his tie-less appearance was the cause. But in an instant, he recognized the expression in Alan Stirling's face: the Yale law professor waiting for the answer to a tricky question.

'I'll start with the Galantine of Boar's Head with Pistachios and Whole Grain Mustard Chantilly,' he began, reading every word slowly and precisely. Sybil stiffened; she knew exactly what that meant. 'Then I'll have the Endives Salad' – he pronounced it 'ahn-deev' the French way, for which he received a gentle kick under the table – 'but bring it with the entrée: I'll have the Rack of Venison with the Brussels sprouts.' The waiter was midway in a second attempt at bowing to Alan Stirling when Arturo continued. 'Do you happen to have chestnut puree? Chestnuts go rather well with game, don't you think, Mr Stirling?' he asked his neighbour, trying to ignore another nudge under the table.

'I'm not much of a game eater,' replied Sybil's father in an even voice and ordered squab with black truffle butter. Arturo is overdoing it, thought Sybil, and rang up another point in her father's favour.

The waiter was about to collect the menus when he was stopped by Stirling's cheerful question: 'Who wants to join me in a soufflé for dessert? We'd better order it now if we want to make it to the theatre.'

'I can't possibly, Alan,' replied his wife.

'I can't either, Daddy,' added Sybil. 'I've gone off sweets. I'm sure Arturo will join you.'

This time the shoeless touch under the table was a request, not admonishment. Arturo smiled at her. He was prepared to take the hint, but in his own way. 'Sure I'll join you. What kind of soufflé do you prefer, sir?'

'You pick it,' replied her father.

'What kinds of soufflé do you have?' inquired Arturo of the waiter.

'Any kind you wish,' replied the man haughtily, 'Chocolate, strawberry, Grand Marnier, chestnut ...'

Touché, thought Sybil.

Arturo paused as if he were weighing the choices. 'Just those?' he asked. 'Why don't we have Soufflé Harlequin? How does that appeal to you, sir?' he said turning to Sybil's father. Before giving him a chance to reply, he continued, 'I think you'd like it, sir, provided,' he glanced up at the perplexed waiter, 'your chef makes a good Harlequin.' The last word was pronounced with such élan, in such meticulous French, as not to brook any question by the waiter, who retreated wordlessly.

Sybil didn't know whether to laugh or to put on her shoe in preparation for another kick. Her father settled the matter.

'What's Soufflé Harlequin?' he asked with genuine curiosity.

Arturo realized his advantage and decided not to overdo it. 'It's easy to describe but difficult to make. One half is Grand Marnier and the other chocolate. The trick is not to let the two run together. It's like a harlequin's costume, two very distinct colours. And the tastes do complement each other. You'll like it, sir.' In spite of too many 'sirs', Sybil made the score 3-1.

Alan Stirling caught the *maître d*'s eye in the distance. 'This gentleman will pick the wine,' he said when the man reached their table. 'Would you mind?'

Conversation stopped while Arturo studied the wine list. The silence became ponderous. Come on, *amor*, Sybil begged silently, let's get this over with. Arturo felt that two wines were needed to demonstrate his oenological prowess. Never mind the price, he thought, this is on Sybil's father. He turned the pages slowly, well aware of the father's scrutiny and the *maître d*'s supercilious patience. Arturo's first inclination was to order Californian wines, but then he decided on a geopolitical compromise.

'We'll start with the Chalone Chardonnay, the '79 Private Reserve.' Silently he shuddered at the price. Chalone was one of the top California wineries when it came to distinctive Chardonnays, but the price was still outrageous. 'With the entree, bring us a bottle of the '82 Château Palmer. And open it right away; it'll need some time to breathe.'

Sybil made the score 3-2. She'd caught on to all but two nuances of this performance: she was unaware of the absurd price of the Palmer and the fact that 1982 was one of the greatest years for Bordeaux.

The next hour made Sybil lose all apprehension. She'd always known Arturo as a superb conversationalist and he didn't disappoint her now. During the meal it became obvious that her father was impressed. The elder Stirling didn't even flinch when he learned that Arturo Flores wasn't half-way up some corporate law firm ladder, but rather a partner in a public advocate firm specializing in problems of farmworkers, migrant labourers, Central-American political immigrants, and the like. Sybil wasn't sure who deserved this round, but since she didn't have to defend her judgment in public, she evened the score.

'Look,' her father exclaimed. 'I think this is for us!'

Sybil and Arturo turned to see a white-capped chef, followed by an entourage consisting of *maître d'*, waiter and bus-boy, approaching the table with a soufflé dish supported on two crisp starched napkins. 'Your Soufflé Harlequin, Mr Stirling,' the chef pronounced formally, while presenting the dish for Sybil's father's inspection. 'You're only the second person in my five years at St Honoré's who has ordered one.'

'It looks beautiful,' replied Stirling, 'but you should show it to Mr Flores. He's the one who picked it.'

The chef turned toward the younger man, whom he had not even deigned to notice until now. He stared at Arturo's open shirt.

'It looks perfect,' remarked Arturo. 'The Baur-au-Lac couldn't have done better. Let's see whether it tastes as good as it looks.'

'The Baur-au-Lac?' Alan Stirling and the chef had

pronounced these words in unison. Sybil's father burst out laughing, but to the chef these words were clearly a magic password.

'So that's why you ordered this soufflé, sir? I should've known. That's where I learned to make it.' It was the first friendly remark that any staff member of St Honoré's had directed to Arturo. In Sybil's silent score-keeping Arturo had finally moved into the lead.

'Where's the Baur-au-Lac?' This time Mr and Mrs Stirling spoke simultaneously and for once unseemly loud laughter reverberated in the subdued dining-room.

'It's a hotel in Zurich. Soufflé Harlequin is their dessert speciality,' announced Arturo.

Sybil made no attempt to hide her surprise. '*Amor*, how on earth did you know that?'

Arturo was enjoying the attention; he'd caught the glance the Stirlings had exchanged when they'd heard Sybil's *amor*. '*Chulita*, there are a couple of things you don't know about me. The Baur-au-Lac is one of them.'

After coffee, the waiter – by now totally confused about the identity of the host – placed the bill discreetly in neutral territory in the middle of the table. Nearly ten minutes passed in amiable conversation with neither man making any move toward it. Gradually, Arturo started to worry: why had Sybil's father not picked up the bill?

His nervousness did not diminish when Sybil turned to her mother. 'I'm glad you and Daddy joined us for dinner. We'd better go to the powder room before we leave for the theatre. There's bound to be a long line there.'

Madre mía', thought Arturo. Am I going to be stuck with this bill? A quick calculation convinced him that the dinner bill alone would far exceed two hundred dollars, even without the wine or tip. He knew exactly how much the Chalone and Palmer bottles cost – and he was the only one of the four who did. Slowly it dawned on him that he might get stuck with the most expensive restaurant meal of his life.

His arithmetic was interrupted by Sybil's father rising from his chair. 'Arturo,' he said – the younger man's preoccupation with money made him miss the gesture of intimacy, of inclusion into the family – 'I'm going to stop at the men's room before we take off for the theatre.'

As soon as Stirling had departed, Arturo glanced around furtively. Without moving his head, he lifted the edge of the paper resting face down in no-man's land, the way a poker player examines the last card dealt, and dropped it with a shudder. What the hell, he thought, I might as well test *el padre*. Quickly he wrote a cheque for $595.76. In his excitement, he even miscalculated the tip, but he did have time to wonder what the peculiar seventy-six cents balance was. He signalled to the waiter, who stood in the distance observing the scene. 'Take this cheque,' said Arturo in an uncharacteristically ingratiating voice, 'but don't mention that I've already paid for the meal.'

Without looking at the folded cheque, the waiter nodded. Had it not been for his self-absorption, Arturo might have noticed the faint smile. But he wouldn't have guessed its cause: three minutes earlier, just around the entrance to the dining-room, the waiter had accepted from Alan Stirling six crisp one-hundred dollar bills accompanied by the comment 'Keep the change, but don't mention that I've paid the bill.'

Arturo Flores was not a stingy man. In fact, within

the fairly circumscribed limits of his income, one could call him generous. But spending nearly 600 dollars on dinner depressed him. Some of his clients didn't earn that much in a month. As Sybil and her mother returned, she was surprised to see a sombre Arturo, chin in hand, staring into space. As far as she could tell, the bill resting on the table was still untouched. Soon they were joined by her father, who promptly startled them with a joke. Sybil was puzzled. Her father wasn't a joke teller. Was this his way of making Arturo feel at ease? If so, her father's behaviour had the opposite effect: Arturo's laughter definitely sounded forced. Meanwhile, the bill seemed glued face down to the tray on which it rested, as if invisible to both men. She looked at her watch. In a minute they'd have to leave for the theatre. A glance at her mother showed that she'd also noticed the lonely, undisturbed bill. Suddenly, Arturo turned toward her parents. 'The theatre is only a ten minute walk from here and it's all downhill. If you're willing to walk, we should start.'

'A first class idea,' exclaimed the father. 'It will settle our soufflé. Marian is a great walker, so let's go.' His wife gazed at the bill and then at her daughter, who returned the questioning look with a discreet gesture toward the same object, now the centrepiece of the table.

Arturo moved behind Sybil's chair. 'Let's go,' he said with an impatient edge. Marian Stirling, visibly irritated, reached for the bill, but the waiter stopped her. 'Excuse me, Madame,' he said as he deftly extracted the folded piece of paper from her hand, 'this dinner is on the house.' Turning to Arturo he added, 'That's a very elegant ascot you're wearing, sir.'

THE DACRIOLOGIST

'Excuse me, please,' Jasper Gunderson mumbled as he made his way through the crowd. 'Excuse me.' He'd never been to a vernissage – he hadn't known the word when Bruce Rosen had first mentioned it – and when he'd found out from the invitation that it was only an opening, he'd almost decided not to come. Contemporary art was not exactly Gunderson's forte. At the front desk he'd seen a price list of Rosen's oils and watercolours. Most were in the 9000-17,000 dollars range. My God, thought Gunderson, I didn't know Rosen was in that class. Pushing through the jammed gallery, without even a drink in his hand, he was looking for just one painting. *Pat in Tears* was number 14, NFS. It was, he noticed, the only one not for sale.

Number 14 was in the side gallery, where the crowd was smaller. Patricia's portrait was a large oil – so large that the couple with their backs against it blocked its view only partly. It was a light grey canvas with the faintest outline of a human figure. Gunderson saw, after a moment, that the woman in the painting was shedding tears. She was not supposed to be crying, Gunderson was sure: something about the expression on her face told him she was only shedding tears. He felt as if Patricia were about to tiptoe from the mysteriously grey canvas into the bright room.

The woman was first to turn around when she noticed Gunderson trying to navigate around them.

'God, Chuck. Take a look! And we were standing right in front of it.' She smiled at Gunderson. 'Aren't these gallery openings terrible? We don't even pay attention to what's here. I guess you do, though, don't you?'

'I don't usually come to such events.' The confession made Gunderson sound like an outsider. He decided to make up for it by some subtle upstaging. 'I only wanted to see this portrait. Isn't it remarkable how Rosen almost forces Patricia to come at you if you keep your eyes on her?'

'Patricia?' The man walked to the wall to read the label. 'She sure is weeping.'

'How do you know?' Gunderson asked sharply.

'What do you mean, how do I know? I can see tears. All you've got to do is look long enough.'

'Just because you see tears doesn't mean a person is weeping.'

'Wait a moment, Chuck,' interjected the woman. 'Weeping implies unhappiness. What the man meant was that just because you see some tears doesn't mean the woman was unhappy. Isn't that so?'

'Exactly,' replied Gunderson. 'That's what I meant.'

'By the way, I am Valerie Hemming and this is Chuck Philpott.'

'My name is Gunderson,' he said, shaking her proffered hand. He'd deliberately omitted his first name, he wasn't ready yet to 'Chuck' her friend, or whatever Philpott was.

'What's your first name?'

'Jasper,' he admitted.

'So why is she crying?' Philpott asked.

Gunderson stared at the painting. Without taking his eyes off Patricia, he said, 'She was moved by something that she'd heard.'

Valerie broke a silence. 'How do you know?'

'I can feel it.'

An awkward quiet had fallen over them when a cheerful voice intervened. 'So you did come, Jasper. I wasn't sure whether you'd make it – you don't usually leave your lab this early. Well, what do you think of your star subject?'

'It's mesmerizing, Bruce. Do you know these people? This is Valerie ...' The usual blank descended over Gunderson, but Philpott saved him.

'I'm Chuck Philpott. You must be Bruce Rosen.'

Hands were shaken all around.

'We were just wondering why this woman is shedding tears,' Valerie said. 'Did I put it the right way, Mr Gunderson, "shedding tears"? Is that precise enough?'

The grin disarmed Gunderson. 'Quite.'

'Mr Rosen,' continued Valerie, 'you tell us: what caused Patricia's tears?'

Rosen looked amused. 'Why ask me? You're talking to one of the world's authorities, and Patricia was one of Dr Gunderson's favourite experimental subjects. Isn't that true, Jasper? But I've got to go into the main gallery. There are lots of people I still have to greet.'

'Are you a physician?' Philpott had turned deferential.

'No,' replied Gunderson. 'I'm a dacriologist.' He said it dead-pan, expecting the usual question.

For once, he was disappointed. Before Philpott even had a chance to ask, Valerie interrupted. 'Are you a soft or a hard dacriologist?'

'What on earth are you people talking about?' asked Philpott.

A triumphant smile was on Valerie's face. '*Dakrios*, Greek for tear.'

'Valerie! How come you know this?'

'I majored in classics before going to Wharton,' she said without looking at Philpott. Her hand was on Gunderson's arm. 'Well, what's your answer?'

Gunderson enjoyed the unexpected repartee. He'd taken Valerie for a gregarious yuppie. 'What's the distinction?' he asked. Sexual innuendos had never before been part of his professional introduction.

'Oh, you know, Jasper.' He liked the bantering way in which she addressed him by his first name. 'Are you interested in the psychological reasons for tears, or do you study their composition?'

'I guess I'm a hard dacriologist with some soft undertones.'

'In that case, let's have dinner together,' said Valerie.

In the elevator, Gunderson turned to Valerie. 'Do you always invite men you've just met to dinner? And shouldn't you have included Philpott? I had the feeling he wasn't very happy we took off so suddenly.'

Valerie just shrugged. 'Chuck's a bore. Besides, I'm surrounded by MBA types all day long …'

'Aren't you one? You mentioned having gone to Wharton.' Gunderson felt unexpectedly relaxed. And curious.

'I sure am.' She grinned. 'That's why I invited you: I want to know what makes a dacriologist tick.'

'Tick?' Gunderson produced a frown. 'What an analytical word!'

'That's the problem with MBAs – we pretend to be analytical, but we're just nosy. But how did you get into tears? I'm fascinated by them.'

'It's not the sort of word I usually hear in reference to tears.'

'Do you like Indian food?'

'I've hardly eaten any,' replied Gunderson.

'Then I'll take you to Bikash's. It's just the place for a dacriologist.'

Jasper Gunderson had been single for several years. This state suited him – a number of fleeting romances, two serious liaisons, but nothing lasting. A dacriologist meets many women, but he has to be careful not to mix his professional and romantic lives. Patricia Maxwell might have become an exception, but then she'd moved in with Bruce Rosen, and he'd become friends with both. Right now, he was in one of those in-between stages when his personal antennae were particularly sensitive to women.

As Valerie discussed the dinner choices with the Sikh waiter, Gunderson had his first opportunity to examine her at leisure. She was a striking woman, who needed little make-up and evidently knew it: smooth, sun-tanned skin; a lower lip periodically moistened by the tip of her tongue; grey eyes, which perpetually seemed amused; and brown hair, with a bleached streak, cut so dashingly short on the sides and at the back as to border on punk. Altogether a daring arrangement for an MBA.

But what had appealed particularly to Gunderson was the woman's almost mannish self-assurance, which he had first noticed at the gallery. Then, she insisted that they use her car – a two-seater Triumph – with the top down. No sooner had he closed the door when she had announced, 'I don't want to argue at the end of the meal about who'll pay. Tonight, you are my guest.'

'We'll start with samosas and masala popadum,' she said to the waiter. 'Then let's have chicken pall and the prawn vindaloo ... and bring us also some chapati.' She scanned the menu. 'We've got to have some vegetables. How about some small portions of spinach bhaji and aloo sag bhaji? And some rice: the zaffarani chawal.' The Sikh nodded. 'Jasper,' she asked, 'have you ever drunk lassi? Let's be completely Indian tonight.'

'I've never even heard of it.'

'Good,' she said. 'In that case we'll order one salty and one sweet. This way you can experiment. And you'd better bring us some ice water,' she continued, addressing the waiter. The Sikh smiled and left.

Valerie leaned across the table. 'Jasper, now tell me what you meant – about being a hard dacriologist with soft undertones. I like the description – I might borrow it sometime and replace "dacriologist" with "MBA".'

'Would you really like to hear the whole story? How I started as an analytical biochemist, developing methods for detecting bodily trace constituents?' He'd assumed a faintly mocking professorial style, but Valerie was having none of it.

'Just make it short and pithy. How did you get into tears?'

Gunderson stopped playing with the chutney dish. 'I couldn't resist the challenge of examining tears once I'd heard – six years and a couple of hundred volunteers ago – that we know less about their composition than about that of any other physiological liquid. It took a long time just to establish the composition of basal tears – the ones we produce all the time, that never run down our cheeks. I used two techniques, capillary gas chromatography and mass spectrometry …'

'Come on, Jasper, get to the point!'

Gunderson looked startled. 'In addition to classics, have you also studied chemistry?'

'Of course not. But you're telling me about your work as a hard dacriologist. What I want to know is the soft side: what's all this chemistry leading to?'

Keeping his hands occupied was one of Gunderson's idiosyncracies at meal times. He started to draw lines in the condensation on the water glass. 'By now, I can map virtually all organic compounds in a tear so that I get the equivalent of chemical fingerprints.'

'You mean each person has unique tears?'

Gunderson turned the glass around to find some unused surface for his doodling. 'On the contrary, tears are pretty similar, even though the fingerprints are fairly complex. Our methods are so refined that we can detect the smallest traces – parts per trillion – of organic compounds. One day we found a difference between tears from male and female subjects. Tears from men contained metabolites of the male sex hormone, testosterone, whereas in women – depending on the time of their menstrual cycle – we encountered varying amounts of estrogenic and progestational hormone derivatives.'

His companion looked impressed, the way laymen do at times when scientists pontificate. 'Jasper, don't tell me you can tell from a woman's tears whether she is pregnant.'

'Not yet. We haven't looked at enough different tear samples from pregnant women. But your question gets close to my interest in "soft" dacriology. I asked myself: if one can detect traces of sex hormones, what about other chemicals that are associated with mood changes? Hormones like adrenaline or steroids related to cortisone, which are produced under stress; substances like serotonin and other psychogenic factors. I figured that if we could accomplish that, analysis of tears might offer some insight into their origin – at the very least, whether they are tears of happiness and laughter or of grief and pain.'

'And can you do this?' asked Valerie.

'We're well on the way,' replied Gunderson. 'What we need is data on many more volunteers.'

'How do you collect the tears? How do you know whether the tears are indeed produced when the person was joyful or depressed? How do you …?'

Gunderson raised his hands. 'Did you invite me for dinner or for a crash course in dacriology?'

'Both,' she said. 'But here comes the appetizer. I'll give you some rest while we eat the samosas and you try the lassi.'

Gunderson took his time chewing. It gave him a moment to decide whether he should tell Valerie about Patricia Maxwell. Why not? he thought. It was Patricia that introduced me to Valerie.

'Let me start with Patricia Maxwell, whose portrait you saw in the gallery. She was one of the first subjects – when we were still establishing base line values under controlled conditions in the laboratory. We were looking for individuals who had a facility for lacrimation, who could easily put themselves into a tearfully depressed or elevated mood, and who'd be prepared to jot down what had made them cry at that moment. Incidentally, we always collect tears from each eye, so as to have two samples for each episode.'

'You know, Jasper,' Valerie said, 'making your

patients "tearfully depressed" doesn't sound like a great thing to do to them. Or don't you call them patients?'

'No, we don't. They're not sick. Anyway, this is where Patricia came in. In the mood lab, within minutes, she could put herself into a happy or unhappy state and the tears would come pouring out.'

'Mood lab?'

'It's a small room with a couple of comfortable chairs, a VCR, a record player with earphones, and a good reading light; that's all. We use videotapes, music, or books to get people into different moods that produce tears. We have them collect the tears and then define their mood numerically, on a mood thermometer ...'

'You must be kidding. Is there such a thing?'

There were times when Gunderson hated to be questioned about his research methods – especially the 'soft' ones. Every time he passed the mood lab and heard muffled sobbing or screams of laughter, he shuddered. Can a biochemist call this research? It always took some effort to sound convincing when he asked his subjects to complete a 'Profile of Mood States' – a self-rating scale with lots of adjectives from which the psychogenic reasons for lacrimation could be deduced. Or the 'Beck Depression Inventory', which at least sounded more clinical. Still, all they gave him was words, and he wanted numbers. So he came up with the thermometer.

'It's just an arbitrary scale, from zero to one hundred. You'd have to be deliriously happy to measure one hundred and hopelessly depressed to rate zero. The numerical ratings are based on special questionnaires that our subjects complete right after we've finished collecting tears.'

Valerie was listening with her elbows on the table, chin in her hands. 'Go on.'

'Well – Patricia was phenomenal. She could switch from one mood into another within minutes. Her tear composition was unbelievably reproducible. Once we'd picked up the presence of certain psychogenic chemicals in tears, we moved out of the mood lab into the field. Here, look at this.' Jasper fished out of his pocket a small cellophane envelope. 'This is a type of surgical sponge that we give to our field volunteers. These are people – mostly women, I have to admit – who are willing to contribute tears whenever they happen to cry. All we ask of the women is not to wear any make-up near the eyes and to gently dab any excess tears with this absorbent wad, put it into the envelope and label it. The only other thing we request is that they measure their mood as soon as feasible on our thermometer scale. What we are trying to do is to accumulate a library of different chemical fingerprints – we call them dacriographs – for tears produced under various circumstances.'

Gunderson was vaguely aware that he'd been lecturing, but Valerie didn't seem to mind. He was about to ask whether she wanted to enter his dacriological entourage (as he called his volunteers, though not to their faces), when they were interrupted by the waiter with their food.

'What should I start with? About the only thing I can recognize is the spinach.'

'Try the main dishes, and see which one you prefer,' replied Valerie.

Gunderson dipped into the chicken pall.

'Better taste just a little bit,' Valerie said, but the warning had come too late. Gunderson was about to make a complimentary remark when the first burning sensation registered on his tongue. His next breath simulated bellows that had caught smouldering embers at just the right moment. Gunderson's obvious reflex was to get the burning stuff out of his mouth, but in his panic he chose the wrong direction: he swallowed it. Valerie had covered her mouth with her hand in a gesture of sympathy and to restrain laughter as she watched his eyes bulge and fill with panic. Gunderson drained his glass of water in one swig, but it was like water hitting sauna stones: a puff of steam and momentary cooling, followed by a wave of moist, even more intense heat.

He searched for his handkerchief to wipe away the tears, but stopped before he found it to gulp down his almost untouched glasses of lassi, tasting neither the sweetness nor the salt nor the yoghurt, and feeling only a slight diminution of the fire in his mouth. At that moment the Sikh arrived. Majestically he poured ice water into the glass, and with a moistened napkin wiped Gunderson's brow.

'How could you order something like that?' he gasped after downing his fourth glass.

'I adore spicy food, but I eat the pall with plenty of chapati. See?' she said. 'Like this. Jasper, I'm sorry I did this to you. But chalk it up to professional experience. What do you think your dacriograph would look like if you analysed the tears that you just shed?'

'You've got a point there,' conceded Gunderson. 'There is a rare pathological condition – it's called a gusto-lacrimal reflex – in which a person cries the moment food is tasted. But we haven't bothered to analyse the tears of normal people who eat food like this.' In spite of his smouldering mouth he was grinning. 'I won't touch any other dish until I first see you do it.'

Valerie took a bite of the prawn vindaloo. 'This is very tasty, but not so hot; it's nothing like the pall. Here, try it.'

Sitting back, she asked, 'Would you accept me as a volunteer?'

'Why do you ask?' he said, stalling for time.

'I cry frequently. I try not to let it happen in the office. They'd just consider it a sign of weakness, but there's nothing wrong with a good cry, is there? Tell me,' she continued after a pause, 'have you figured out yet why one gets such a sense of relief after crying?'

Gunderson's mouth was partly open to receive the first prawn, but now he stopped. Using his fork, for emphasis, he resumed his lecturing style. 'There's a man in Minnesota who thinks that shedding tears may be the way whereby the body gets rid of stressful chemicals.'

'Is that true of all crying?'

The fork was swinging in time to Gunderson's shaking head. Both of them noticed the moving prawn and laughed. 'No, certainly not all tears. For instance, I rather doubt that Frey – that's the man in Minnesota – would claim that the tears you saw streaming down my face fell into that category. It was the four glasses, not my tears, that helped me recover from the chicken. No, Frey was only thinking of emotionally stimulated tears – what we call psychogenic weeping. His hypothesis is based primarily on the observation that a subject exposed to freshly sliced onions produces a much smaller volume of tears than when the same person cries because of some emotional stress. But all he'd have to do is to come here ...' He gestured at the chicken pall. 'It's still too early to tell whether tears are nature's disposal system for emotional wastes,' Gunderson rather liked the metaphor, 'but maybe we'll be able to provide some evidence for Frey's hypothesis.'

'So now,' Valerie said, 'you are collecting dacriographs to see whether you can tell why people were crying, rather than to determine what the function of tears is?'

'Precisely.'

'Well, in that case I want a bunch of your sponges and some of your emotional check forms. I'd like to run my own test. I'd like to check your' – she paused for a moment – 'dacriological prowess before I make a commitment as a volunteer.'

In the weeks following their dinner, Valerie provided several carefully labelled envelopes – the dates as well as the hours of tear collection were marked clearly – but she withheld the mood thermometer ratings and completed Profile of Mood State forms. This was, her note read, to test the validity of Gunderson's dacriographs. He accepted the challenge, partly out of professional pride and partly because such circumstances justified his maintaining a social relationship with Valerie. She could hardly be considered an ordinary subject if she was unprepared to follow the standard protocol.

The first five samples came out well. Gunderson correctly identified two samples as 'happy' – Valerie had given them a 75 and 82 rating on the mood thermometer scale – and three as 'depressed' ones. He even provided an impressive example of subdivision: one of the dacriographs had shown several characteristic 'rage' peaks, whereas the other two fell into the conventional 'sad' category.

One day Valerie called after lunch to announce that

she would stop at the Wet Eye Institute to deliver a new sample. The first time Jasper had mentioned the name of his laboratory, Valerie had laughed. Mildly irritated, Gunderson had pointed out that 'there is a Dry Eye Institute in Texas' – although he had refrained from adding that it was in the apparently unlikely location of Lubbock – 'which studies various pathological states associated with excess drying of the eye.' He had added, in a moment of scientific one-upmanship, that even the use of oral contraceptives had been found to affect tear volume.

'I brought you a special sample, collected early this morning. I'll be interested in what you find.' They were in his small office, adjacent to the laboratory. Gunderson offered to show her around his professional empire – he was anxious to impress her – but Valerie refused.

'Some other time,' she said. 'I've got to get back to the office and you've got to analyse my tears.'

Valerie's latest dacriographs did not appear in Gunderson's office until three days later. The day before, he'd sensed a strange disappointment in Valerie's voice on the telephone when she discovered that her tears had not yet been processed.

To expedite his examination of dacriographs – he had daily to look at dozens of them – he'd made some templates of certain standard ones, which had all of the characteristic chemical peaks associated with 'happy' or 'unhappy' crying, including some of the subdivisions that he'd been able to establish. As a matter of policy, Gunderson never scanned labelled dacriographs – he didn't want to be prejudiced in his evaluation. Only after he'd compared one particular graph with all of his standard templates and been struck by the presence of two peaks that he'd never observed before, did he discover that it had come from Valerie's left eye. Half an hour later, he encountered a second such anomalous sample with the same extra peaks – from Valerie's right eye. It was standard practice in his lab to mix the dacriographs of tears from the right and left eyes of one subject with all the other graphs. This offered an independent check of the validity of his analytical procedure: to see whether he could pick out the two matching samples from a large pile.

'Valerie? Where did the last sample come from?' It was only the second time that he'd telephoned her at the office. There was no chit-chat. 'There was something peculiar about the two dacriographs.'

'Why blame me?' she asked kiddingly, but with a note of pride.

'Can you get me another such sample? We'd like to check it again and see whether we can identify these new peaks.'

'So I have new peaks? Yes, I can bring you a new sample.'

'How soon?'

Valerie hesitated. 'I'm in a meeting now. Let's see. Maybe tonight. Late tonight. Actually the morning is preferable. Yes; tomorrow morning. I'll drop them off on my way to the office.'

This time, Valerie's new specimens did not end up on the bottom of the pile. Gunderson had left instructions at the front desk to have Valerie bring them personally to his office. But Valerie didn't appear. The receptionist brought an envelope containing the two samples and a note: *Jasper – Call me when you have analysed these, but not at my office. Ciao, Val.*

Only once had Gunderson been told to his face that

some of his volunteers actually resented his ability to identify their moods from their tears. Patricia Maxwell had explained to him how his tear experiments had initially intrigued her; how she'd enjoyed contributing to his original analytical studies. But when he started to define her moods in chemical terms, she'd felt a sense of intrusion which Bruce Rosen shared. 'Listen, Jasper, I can't come back to your lab,' she'd said. 'I don't want my mood defined chemically. Bruce never questions me about my tears, but you should see the portrait he's just painted of me. My feelings are all there, but I don't feel violated.' Now he wondered whether Valerie's unwillingness to appear personally with her latest tear samples was related to Patricia's earlier feelings.

This time Gunderson analysed Valerie's samples himself and found that the two new peaks were even more intense. He spent the rest of the morning refining the data.

'Valerie, I know that you didn't want me to call you at the office. But I've just analysed your last two samples myself and I think I'm on the right track. Can I quickly ask you a couple of questions?'

'I guess so,' she said, with an impatience that didn't seem quite genuine. 'But make it quick, I'm in a meeting.'

'Valerie ...' Jasper hesitated. 'Have you by any chance just gone on oral contraceptives?'

'What?' she broke out laughing.

'Did you just start on the Pill?'

'Why, Dr Gunderson! What a question to ask at three in the afternoon in my office.'

'Come on, Valerie; be serious. The peaks in your tears are unusual steroid metabolites, which might have come from one of the new types of Pills. Your first five samples didn't show them.'

'I'm sorry to disappoint you, doc.' She lowered her voice. 'I've been on the same Pill for five years. Nice try, Jasper.'

'Oh.' Gunderson's disappointment was palpable. 'Just one more question. At what point in your menstrual cycle are you right now?'

After a pause, she replied, 'The end of the first week.' She added, 'I'll call you tonight, but it will be late. I've got a business engagement this evening.'

When the telephone rang, Gunderson was conducting the third movement of the 'Death of a Maiden' quartet with one hand and with the other slowly turning the pages of the latest issue of *Biochimica et Biophysica Acta*.

Valerie said, 'I can hear you're not yet asleep. What are you playing?'

'Schubert,' he said. 'Valerie, can you produce such tears at will?'

'Almost.'

'Can you do it anytime?'

'Theoretically, yes.'

'What does that mean?' persisted Gunderson.

'It means just what it says. In theory, I could cry like this at any time, but in practice I don't.'

'Does another person's actions cause your tears?'

'No,' she said after a pause, 'not necessarily.'

'OK, enough of guessing. I give up. Tell me how these tears are produced.'

'Produced?' she echoed. 'What an analytical word. I guess it's only appropriate that I resolve this mystery of science for you at dinner. I'll cook it at my place, but I can't do it until Saturday evening.'

The evening was superb. The food was mild and

sophisticated; nothing spicy; more an American version of *nouvelle cuisine*. The apartment was furnished in modern Italian – not yuppie Scandinavian. There were several *avant garde* prints on the walls, one large abstract oil, and lots of books; some of the economics titles were almost as incomprehensible to him as the Greek ones. There were leather-bound volumes of Ovid, Virgil and Catullus, and an entire shelf of French literature. 'Do you also know French, in addition to your Greek and Latin?' he asked as she came out of the kitchen with an open bottle of wine.

'*Mais oui, Monsieur Jaspér,*' she replied, accenting his name on the last syllable and rolling the 'r' softly.

They were sitting on the sofa, sipping port and listening to Berg's 'Lyric Suite'. The only light was that of the four candles on the dining-room table. Valerie, shoeless, was leaning against one corner of the sofa in her simple white silk kimono and pants, a black belt tied around her waist, karate style. 'Content?' she asked, raising her glass.

'Content,' said Gunderson. 'But not satisfied. What about those tears?'

Valerie slid toward him, took the glass out of his hand and kissed him. She was naked under her silk garment, and not in a mood for foreplay; Gunderson had barely realized what was transpiring when he found himself on his back, with Valerie thrusting on top of him. Her torso was arched backwards, her hands firmly clasping Jasper's outspread legs, until she collapsed on him with her gasps loud, her tears wetting his neck.

Castor's Dilemma

Professor I. Castor knew perfectly well that he was eligible for a Nobel Prize – in fact, during the past couple of years, the subject had never been far from his mind. He was quite aware that timing was critical: if he were to win the Prize, it would have to happen during the next three, or at most four, years, while his field was still red-hot.

In the cancer field, a generalized theory of tumour production is Mt Everest. Only superstars climb Everest, and I. Castor was such a superstar. One day, he had a spectacular idea about tumorigenesis – the kind that a scientist gets once, or if fantastically lucky, twice in a lifetime, like Watson and Crick's double helix. Even more importantly, he conceived of an experiment – a bold approach to his Everest – that would unambiguously convert his theory into fact.

Castor still remembered the day, just a few months before, when he stepped out of the interminable fog of discarded theories into the sudden sunlight of an idea which he felt intuitively to be right. All he needed was one successful experiment, and he had the man to do it: Jeremiah P. Stafford, who had only recently obtained his Ph.D. degree in Castor's lab.

Usually, Castor was both informal and comfortable with his star student. This time, however, the professor did not look at him, but past him – at the blackboard behind Stafford's back.

'I've never before asked you to drop an experiment in midstream, but I'm going to do it now.' Castor looked expectantly at the young man, but Stafford offered no response. With Stafford, it had become a game not to show any expression during these scientific *tête-à-têtes*. Much as he revered his mentor, he always imagined himself in a subtle battle of strength in which he defended some private territory that Castor would not be allowed to penetrate.

'Furthermore,' Castor's eyes had again begun to wander, 'I'd like you not to talk to anybody about what I'll tell you.' He quickly glanced at Stafford. This time, Castor had won a point: the young man's surprise was all too evident. Though fiercely ambitious, Castor loved to talk about his ideas to peers, colleagues and students, and never worried about getting scooped. The professor's openness was legendary. No wonder bright graduate students competed for the few available spaces in his laboratory. But for once, Castor had kept his mouth shut. He had not brought up his new theory in his weekly research seminar, nor had he called Karl Krauss, the Harvard cancer doyen, who even had a sarcoma named after him. He'd picked only one confidant and Stafford appreciated the magnitude of the compliment.

Thrilled, Stafford grabbed some paper and scribbled notes as he listened to the outline of the experiment and the plan of attack. Castor felt that the experiment could be done in less than three months.

'Jerry, you do understand why I want this experiment to be kept quiet, don't you? This is not the usual "if" experiment. This experiment will be in all the textbooks; it's the sort you encounter once in a lifetime. Look how lucky you are: it's taken me over fifty years, while you …'

Castor's voice trailed off as he gazed at his young collaborator with affection and a tinge of envy. Stafford was his all-time favourite student, and to that extent deserved this chance. But what a chance it was! If only he had been offered such an opportunity at the age of twenty-six!

When Castor resumed, it was business as usual. 'Jerry, you do know what's at stake here? Let's go to work.'

In less than two months Stafford produced the expected results. Castor was triumphant. He stayed up all night writing the first draft of the brief communication to be published in *Nature* – the most widely read journal in his field. The paper's authors were I. Castor and J.P. Stafford. According to Castor, the order was purely alphabetical, but one of the laboratory cynics had wondered why there were never any Allens or Browns in the group. There had been an exchange fellow from Prague, named Czerny, but that was the closest alphabetical proximity to Castor that had occurred.

'A Generalized Theory of Tumorigenesis' was promptly accepted for publication. When the *Nature* article appeared, even Castor was staggered by the number of reprint requests. The colleague he respected most – Karl Krauss from Harvard – called to say that this paper could not possibly escape notice in Stockholm.

'I. C., if I were an envious man, I'd now be bright green. But you know I'm not.' His chuckle sounded almost convincing. 'If I couldn't think of this experiment, then at least I'm glad you did.'

Castor could feel the warm blush spill over his face. It wasn't due to embarrassment; just sheer pleasure. Krauss's Harvard was a place that counted Nobel laureates almost by the dozen. However, at Castor's mid-western university, only one Nobel Prize had ever been won, and that was in the nineteen-thirties. Getting a Nobel five decades later would put I.C. in a class all by himself. You couldn't do that at Harvard or Berkeley!

At such moments, scientific etiquette demands modesty. But the demure look towards the floor, the disclaimer with the hands, as often as not look faked when seen. The telephone is kinder.

Castor rose to the occasion. 'Karl, I knew it was a good idea' – *good? It was the greatest idea I've ever had!* – 'but I was also lucky. I've told you before about Jeremiah Stafford. The guy has golden hands – you've never seen such lab technique. I don't know if anyone else could've pulled this off.'

For three months, Castor basked on the summit of his Everest – lectures, seminars, and symposia – where he presented *our* experiment. Was it a royal we or a true plural? One never knows with a scientist, who is taught in graduate school never to use the first person singular, even in the absence of any co-workers.

One afternoon, Karl Krauss telephoned to say that one of his best associates ('You remember him, I. C., don't you? He's my Stafford') had been unable to replicate Stafford's experiment. Such a failure was not unheard of in their field. After all, Castor and Stafford had only published a preliminary paper, without presenting experimental details. Castor asked Stafford to prepare a precise description of the laboratory protocols so that they could be sent promptly to Harvard. Stafford agreed.

Within a couple of days, Stafford, who had never missed a day in four years of graduate school, called the professor's secretary rather than Castor.

'Stephanie, please tell I. C. that I caught the flu. I feel so lousy, I don't even want to explain to him why I can't prepare the report for Krauss just now.'

The message annoyed Castor. Stafford, who had taken immediately to the eighty-hour work weeks in Castor's laboratory; who pronounced the word 'vacation' with a disdain born out of scientific machismo; whom Castor had always found in the laboratory – this Stafford had to pick *this* time to feel ill. Castor's annoyance escalated to real irritation when, a few days later, he was told that Stafford had telephoned from Florida: his grandfather had suffered a heart attack. 'Where the hell is the man's loyalty?' he thought. 'To his grandfather, or to the lab project?'

Such gracelessness was not typical of Castor, but he was under some pressure because one did not keep Krauss waiting. This Harvard professor was in a class by himself, and especially so when the validity of a key experiment was in question. Castor decided on a sloppy, but simple short-cut: he would photocopy the appropriate pages from Stafford's laboratory notebook, and send these to Harvard with a brief explanatory letter.

There was nothing improper in copying Stafford's laboratory notebook. In contrast to personal diaries, a scientist's diary is expected to be produced for inspection by others, on demand. Invariably such notebooks are solidly bound, with pre-numbered pages, and all entries are written down chronologically. Like all great expedition leaders, Castor was fanatical about details. Everything had to be entered in the lab notebooks with indelible ink, not pencil; even trivial calculations had to be put into the notebook rather than jotted down elsewhere on loose sheets. Every graduate student starting out got the same speech: 'You can't put too much into your notebook, but you can write too little. You never know which details may turn out to be crucial.' When the students departed from Castor's laboratory, the notebooks stayed behind.

What Castor saw in Stafford's notebook bothered him. The experimental protocol was indeed there, but the precise details seemed surprisingly scant. After some effort, he succeeded in telephoning Stafford in Florida.

'I hope your grandfather is getting better.' Castor left no opening for a reply, because he did not consider it a question. He continued, 'Jerry, you know that Krauss is having one of his postdocs repeat *our* experiment. You know they're having trouble repeating it and I can't let Krauss wait much longer for the experimental details. I thought I'd simply send him Xeroxes of your lab notebook …'

All Castor heard in reply was a low 'Yes?'

'I hadn't looked at your notebook for months …' Castor could not continue, because Stafford had moved promptly onto the offensive.

'Well, you had no reason to do so. Except for our last *Nature* article' – there was no ambiguity about 'our' in this instance – 'you'd asked me to write the first draft of all of our joint manuscripts.'

'Yes, I know.' Whatever accusatory nuance had existed in Castor's earlier tone had now disappeared. Unlike his superstar colleagues, who hardly ever wrote drafts of manuscripts that bore their names as co-authors, Castor, until recently, had always written the first draft. But even he, I. Castor – the superstar who had resisted the temptation of huge research groups in order to have time for scrupulous experimental confirmation and writing – even he had made an exception in recent years with Jeremiah Stafford. This exceptional treatment was only one of several subtle indications that Stafford was being groomed as Castor's successor. Except for Stafford, nobody in the laboratory ever called Castor 'I.C.' to his face. 'Professor Castor' or, on occasion, 'Prof' was established etiquette. Only outsiders or professional equals 'eye-seed' Castor. Nobody remembered when Stafford had joined this select club. It was not that he had been specifically invited; one day he was just there.

Castor was now apologetic. 'Jerry, I can't send just Xerox copies of your notebook pages to Krauss. There are too many missing details. Why, Jerry, you don't even indicate which buffer you used in the original extraction; you don't give the column support for your high-pressure liquid chromatography experiment; you don't say where the arginase came from ...'

Stafford's interruption was peremptory. 'I know, I. C., but these are trivia. This is routine stuff, and you know what time pressure I was working under. Finishing what I did' – the first person singular was verbally underlined – 'in less than three months took some doing. I guess I was just sloppy with my notebook entries. Why don't you let me write up the missing details? I'll be back by Wednesday and you'll have them in your office first thing Friday morning.'

This was what Castor wanted to hear. The letter to Krauss was mailed the following week.

In less than one month, Krauss called to say that his associate, an experienced enzymologist, had still been unable to replicate the key experiment.

Castor's physician had warned him that he'd be

wise to carry nitroglycerine medication with him in case his heart started acting up again. Now Castor reached for his pill box before giving the expected reply: 'Karl, I'll repeat the experiment myself with Stafford. Then, I'll invite your man to come to my lab and do it with us.'

Krauss agreed that this was the most reasonable course; he assured I. C. that until he heard from him, the Harvard group would not publish their failure to repeat what had become known as the 'Castor-Stafford Experiment'. Naming an experiment or theory after the original authors is the ultimate historical accolade in science. However, it is rarely bestowed without eventual independent verification, which Krauss had intended to provide.

Castor immediately summoned Stafford and presented him with the facts: the experiment could not be repeated in Krauss's laboratory. He suspected that a minor but essential experimental variable, not recognized by them, was the reason for their failure. He asked Stafford to perform the experiment with him in his private laboratory. The young man's temporary move into the professor's own laboratory caused considerable comment and even gloating among some members of the research group. After all, Krauss's initial failure to repeat the work outlined in their *Nature* article had not been kept a secret. While none of the students and research fellows had ever been asked to work in Castor's own laboratory, it was hardly a promotion that the professor's fair-haired boy had now been ordered to repeat his spectacular experiment under the watchful eyes of the master.

The weeks passed quickly and without difficulty. Of course, this did not mean much, because everything depended on the final enzyme assay which was due on the following Monday. When Castor arrived in the morning, nervous and concerned, he met an impressively confident and self-assured Stafford. Within a few hours, Castor was in a joyous mood. The assay had come out as expected; the experiment had indeed worked. The professor announced the results at a special group seminar and publicly congratulated his favourite collaborator. He also used the occasion to do a bit of preaching about the importance of laboratory notebook discipline.

When Castor returned to his office, he found a sealed envelope that simply read 'Professor Castor – CONFIDENTIAL'. The message, typed and unsigned, consisted of only one sentence: *Why was Dr Stafford in your private laboratory on Sunday evening?*

It hardly mattered whether unfounded suspicion, bred by professional jealousy, or something more serious had prompted that note. For Castor, the dilemma was enormous. The correct step would have been to call in Stafford, to confront him with the accusation, to repeat the experiment without Stafford, and if he failed in the experiment, to inform Krauss of what had transpired. In addition, he would then have to undergo the expected public penance: a letter published in *Nature*, in which he would withdraw the 'Castor-Stafford Experiment'. The standard ending would be 'pending experimental verification', but everybody would know that fraud was probably involved if Stafford's name was not included in such a letter. If Castor had put on this hair shirt, his tumorigenesis theory would have been just that: one more theory in the cancer field, cast upon an ever-mounting heap of discarded ones. Yet he felt in his bones that his theory had to be right. Even before this disaster, Castor had thought of a second experiment that might provide independent verification. It was risky, but Castor felt that there was now too much at stake – not the least of which was a possible Nobel Prize.

Castor decided to say nothing – neither to Stafford nor to Krauss. By saying nothing, he considered himself still unbesmirched by any possible scandal. Furthermore, instead of wasting precious weeks on another attempted repetition of Stafford's experiment – by thinking of it as 'Stafford's', Castor had already passed mental judgement on the affair – he started on the new experiment, the one he had not mentioned to a soul.

Castor's sudden unavailability stunned his collaborators, but none more so than Stafford. In the past, most students, and certainly Stafford, were privy to what the professor was doing with his own hands. This time, even Stafford's request to see Castor in his laboratory was met by a totally unexpected response from the secretary, who usually just waved Stafford in: 'I'm sorry, Jerry, but Professor Castor is working on a very important experiment. All I can do is take a message.'

Stafford became frantic. He had always had open access to the professor's laboratory; now he was staring at a locked door. This exclusion of Castor's favourite set the lab's rumour mill going full blast. Stafford's anxiety became almost unbearable; he thought of writing a letter, but he wasn't sure what to say in it. Demand an explanation? Give an explanation?

In the end, no letter, nothing, was required. The second experiment – Castor's independent proof of his tumorigenesis theory – did work. He had vindicated his earlier optimism about the viability of his brain-child.

Rather than rushing into print in *Nature*, Castor played it cool and cautious. He telephoned Krauss: it was now unnecessary for the Harvard group to examine further the verification of the 'Castor-Stafford Experiment', because he had just completed a second and experimentally simpler one. In a subtle way, Castor forced Krauss to centre his attention on his own experiment, and away from Stafford's.

'Karl, just wait till you see the details. It's a beauty, but I won't write it up until someone in your lab has repeated *my* work. Before I publish this experiment, I want to be absolutely sure that nobody has problems repeating it. I'll send you Xerox copies of my own lab notebook by Federal Express. You'll get them tomorrow.'

Krauss could not help but agree to become the irreproachable witness to Castor's scientific veracity. What nobody could predict at this time was that Krauss would also spoil Castor's triumph: when the great Krauss eventually published his confirmation of Castor's second experiment – of course, he waited until Castor's triumphant paper had appeared in *Nature* – he referred to that experiment, quite innocently but indelibly, as the 'Castor Confirmation'. For Krauss and every reader, Castor's solo experiment simply confirmed the generalized tumorigenesis theory, whose authors were Castor *and Stafford*.

All this was still in the future. Since Castor was certain that his latest work would be confirmed at Harvard, he had no reason to delay announcing his success through the time-tested laboratory grapevine. He called a special departmental seminar and announced that he would be speaking – without listing a title. Only superstars can use such a ploy. Lesser lights run the risk of an empty room when the notice reads: 'Topic to be Announced.'

In Castor's case, even without the mystery of an untitled talk, his virtual disappearance from public view for weeks would have guaranteed a jammed lecture hall. Stafford deliberately arrived late. As he sat in the back, he was convinced that he was about to witness his own public crucifixion. Shortly after Castor's start, it became obvious that Stafford was not even a participant in the drama about to be presented to the hushed audience. Without referring to Krauss's inability to validate Stafford's work, Castor reported his *second* experimental proof of the generalized tumorigenesis theory. Within hours, the news had spread by long distance telephone to all key laboratories.

In the excitement, nobody had noticed that Stafford had slipped out of the seminar room just as the applause started.

He headed straight for the professor's office. 'Stephanie.' His voice was composed as he sank into a chair in the secretary's office. He acted as if the last few weeks had not existed. 'I. C. just gave the most fabulous talk you could imagine. I just thought I'd wait for him here – I want to tell him what I thought of the seminar.' Stafford did not mind that he had to wait for a long time; he knew that Castor would be surrounded by a throng of admiring students and colleagues at the conclusion of his lecture. It would give him time to rehearse his little speech.

Stafford was still silently debating whether to offer detached congratulations or bubbling enthusiasm when Castor appeared. The young man jumped up. 'Prof' – he did not consider 'I. C.' appropriate under the circumstances, and 'Professor Castor' was clearly too formal – 'could I see you for a moment in your office?' Castor merely looked at his student and then motioned him into the room.

As soon as the door was closed, Stafford switched gears. 'I. C. – I just wanted to see you alone for a moment, because I knew that down in the lecture room you'd be surrounded by everyone. I just wanted to tell you that this was the most fantastic lecture I ever heard. I'd been concerned when I didn't see you for all these weeks, but now I'm relieved.'

The older man's expression did not change. 'You damn well ought to be,' was all he said.

Climbing Everest by two different routes is sensational; hardly anybody has been photographed twice on the summit. This time, Castor's basking there was terminated much quicker than the first time around. Again the message was from Harvard, the bearer Karl Krauss: he congratulated Castor on the brilliant conception of the second experiment and informed him that the verification of Castor's results had already started. Castor felt elated; a potentially devastating situation was well on the way to a permanent resolution.

But then Krauss continued, 'By the way, I. C., your man Stafford called. He asked whether I'd offer him a post-doctorate fellowship in my lab. He said that he'd spent all of his experimental life in your department, and wanted to work on some other problems before looking for an assistant professorship.

'With other people, I wouldn't even have called. But since he's working with you, I wanted to check whether you'd mind if he joined my group. I know your fabulous opinion of Stafford. But you're familiar with our red tape. We need some letters of recommendation in the files, and obviously, one must come from you. Actually, Stafford didn't even list you as a referee; he mentioned that he didn't want to bother you with such a trivial request. In reality, I think he was worried that you might be annoyed that he wants to work in another lab.'

Underneath, Krauss had felt somewhat guilty, which explained this avalanche of words. Now he waited for a response, but none came. For once, Castor was speechless.

His friend mistook the silence for disapproval. He hastened on. 'I. C. – you've got to admit that almost anything the man would do now in your place would be an anti-climax after the spectacular work the two of you published in *Nature*. Could you send me a letter about him? It needn't be long – just write what you've always told me: that he was the best man you've ever had in your lab.'

A monstrous dilemma was now facing Castor. If he refused to send such a letter, he would have to explain the reason to Krauss. After all, I. C. could not just claim that he wanted to keep Stafford around, and therefore would not recommend his best student. But if he did write such a letter, Castor would never again be able to erase the 'Castor-Stafford Experiment' without implicating himself. An enthusiastic letter of recommendation to Krauss would permanently close the door to such a withdrawal. In a flash, Castor realized that Stafford had challenged him with a piece of fiendishly clever blackmail. He decided to pay the ransom, and by May of that year, Stafford had departed for Harvard.

For thirty-five minutes, October 17th could have been called the shortest, best day of Castor's life. I. C. was an early riser, who needed no alarm clock. Shortly after six a.m., while he was showering, the phone rang. Castor had intended to let it ring, but the persistence of the caller finally drove him, dripping wet, to the bed-side phone.

'Professor Isidore Castor?' The man's accented voice was unfamiliar; furthermore, nobody had called Castor 'Isidore' for decades.

He decided to be noncommittal. 'Who's calling?'

'Sven Lundholm from the *Svenska Dagbladet* in Stockholm.'

'Yes?' Castor was barely able to utter this single word, so full of suspense, desire, triumph, and some deviousness. He wanted to pretend cool detachment, but his heart was pounding, so much so that he reached for his nitroglycerine pill box which he always kept by his bed. Every winner had wondered – gratefully, to be sure – why the first call invariably came from a reporter. 'Yes,' he added more forcefully, 'this is Professor Isidore Castor speaking.' (*Isidore Castor? My God, this sounds like a stranger*!). 'What can I do for you?'

'I have the honour to congratulate you on your winning the Nobel Prize in Physiology and Medicine.' Castor did not mind the pompous words; in fact, they had hardly registered. 'I wonder whether you have any comments?'

'Comments? No, I don't. I don't even know whether it's true.' Castor remembered the embarrassment of Vincent Du Vigneaud, who publicly acknowledged his pleasure when a reporter congratulated him prematurely for winning a Nobel Prize. In Du Vigneaud's case, the reporter had been premature by one full year!

'Professor Castor!' The man sounded outraged. 'Surely you do not believe that I am calling from Stockholm to make a joke?'

'How do I know you're calling from Stockholm?' Castor figured he could afford caution, even at the risk of insulting the caller.

'Do you want to call me back in Stockholm?' shot back the reporter. 'I can give you the number of the *Svenska Dagbladet*.'

'Never mind,' replied Castor, who was enjoying himself. 'I'll comment, but for the time being it's off the record.'

'How do you feel having won the Nobel Prize?'

Castor could almost see the reporter rise, as he pronounced the last two words, and bow from the waist. 'Frankly I haven't thought about it, but if it's true, it's a great surprise. If it's true,' he repeated the words for emphasis, 'then it's not just an enormous honour, but also recognition for the efforts of my entire team of collaborators over the years.'

This was the sort of stilted answer that most reporters, even Swedish ones, recognize as fake. The man continued on another tack. 'Professor, what will you do with the prize money? Have you decided how to spend it?'

Castor was taken aback. 'No, of course not. I haven't even thought about it.' This time, the answer was totally correct, but the reporter persisted.

'But you do know how much money goes with the prize?'

Again Castor replied honestly. 'Well, I know it's a lot, but I don't know exactly how much.'

It was a lot of money, but only half of what Castor had imagined. As soon as the Stockholm reporter hung up, Castor turned on the radio to listen to the news. He missed the key words by just a second or two. '...this almost completes an American sweep of this year's Nobel Prizes. Only the one in literature is still to be announced next week.'

'Damn it,' thought Castor. 'Do I have to wait for the seven o'clock news to hear the name, or should I call the radio station?' Actually, he did not have to do anything. The first telephone call followed shortly thereafter. Karl Krauss was on the line.

'I. C.' His voice was warm and excited. Genuine pleasure flowed over the telephone. 'I hope I'm one of the first to congratulate you. You really deserved this Nobel Prize. I'll bet you'll be amused by what I have to tell you. Guess what the announcer said when the Nobel Prize in Medicine was announced this morning over the local Boston station?'

'I haven't got the foggiest idea,' countered Castor.

'Come on,' coaxed Krauss. 'Just guess!'

'OK.' Castor played along with his friend. 'Midwestern cancer whiz wins Nobel.'

'Wrong!' Krauss was triumphant. 'He started out with "another Nobel Prize won by Harvard man". Can you beat our local chauvinism? It's typical of Harvard.'

'I don't get it.' Castor sounded puzzled. 'Why should he have said this?'

'What do you mean, you don't get it? You midwestern yokel! We are so damn anxious to add to our list of Nobel laureates, everybody here is including Stafford on the Harvard roster. Ridiculous, isn't it?'

'Stafford? You mean ...?'

The seeds for the Castor-Stafford combination were probably sown in 1923, when MacLeod and Banting won the Nobel Prize in Physiology and Medicine for Banting's and Best's discovery of insulin. The outcry about the injustice of Professor MacLeod, the director of the laboratory, sharing the Nobel Prize, while young Charles Best, who had performed the crucial experiment, had been ignored, persisted for decades. Since then, the Swedes had almost leaned over backwards to recognize a younger collaborator. In 1983, Milstein and Jerne, together with a much younger Georges Koehler, were only the most recent example of such a shared Nobel Prize; the Castor-Stafford combination probably seemed just to most. After all, the key paper – the one which succinctly, but unequivocally, described the generalized theory of tumorigenesis together with its first experimental proof – had carried the names of both Castor and Stafford.

One of the common courtesies among new Nobel laureates is to congratulate a co-winner, before acknowledging the dozens or even hundreds of congratulatory messages. Yet Castor could not make himself write the conventional letter to Stafford, and strangely, the young man did not contact his mentor.

Like most serious contenders for the Nobel Prize, Castor knew all about the ceremonies: the actual award is presented on an afternoon in early December by the King of Sweden, followed by a spectacular dinner and dance at Stockholm's lovely Town Hall. Later in the week, a major public lecture – subsequently published in book, as well as journal, form – is given by each winner. This lecture, more than anything else, represents the historical record of the winner's scientific immortality.

The weeks before the actual award of the Nobel Prize are clearly the best. Parties, interviews, accolades of every sort, are the usual fare; the novelty has not yet worn off, the prize money has not yet been spent.

Castor had no idea what Stafford was doing, but for I. C. the pressure was building up inexorably. All he could think of was the actual ceremony, when he and Stafford would stand together before the King of Sweden, with the world press and TV covering every detail. But this was nothing compared to Castor's fear of the scientific lecture expected of him and of Stafford. Since both were sharing the Prize for the same discovery, common sense and courtesy would require that they consult each other to decide who would say what, and in which order. But Stafford made no move.

Late one evening in mid-November, after having received a letter from Stockholm asking him to present the first scientific lecture, to be followed by Stafford's, Castor could take the pressure no longer. He sat down at his desk to start on the text of his lecture. Pen in hand, he stared at the empty page for seemingly endless minutes while his heart beat faster and faster. Finally, he reached for his container of nitroglycerine tablets, but to no avail: it was empty. As the pain in his chest became progressively stronger, Castor wrote with a shaking hand the words which subsequently caused such a sensation: 'It is with heavy heart that I ...'

Was this the preamble to his Nobel Prize lecture or to his suicide note? As he set these words on paper, Isidore Castor realized in a flash that it wouldn't make any difference. He wouldn't even make it to the bathroom. For once, there was no dilemma to be resolved.

THE GLYNDEBOURNE HEIST

Name me another opera house where grazing sheep dot the green hills overlooking the place; where the audience, in dinner jackets and evening gowns, arrives from the car park toting chairs, blankets, wicker baskets and tables that would pass muster in many a dining-room; and where some of the real aficionados have already occupied the choice locations – next to the privet hedges or under the huge oaks – to sip champagne and nibble cream cakes, while the cows chew their cud in the adjacent open field across a deep ha-ha.

Glyndebourne is testimony to the British proclivity for pastoral snobbery. It also tests an opera lover's mettle: the long drive or two-hour train and bus ride from London; the need to make reservations months in advance and, for a foreign visitor like me, to be in the country at the right time for the very short season when the summer weather forecasts alternate between 'sunny intervals with occasional showers' and 'rain at first, sunny intervals developing'.

I was myself caught up in the snobbery when I gushed to my host, 'Francis, I can't tell you how impressed I am that you managed to get tickets at such short notice.' Francis Holbrook – stout, pink-cheeked and exuding both affluence and power – beamed as he surveyed the scene of bucolic formality. His son, Nigel, aged twenty-two, who'd come down from Cambridge, was sullen. Purposely, we'd arrived early so that they could show me the gardens before the four-thirty curtain call to *Il Ritorno d'Ulisse in Patria*. We were walking down some stone steps towards an oval lawn in front of a pond surrounded by willows and spotted with water lilies. It looked like a favourite site: elsewhere, people kept their distance while they pulled out tablecloths, cutlery and linen napkins; here in the grassy oval, a dozen groups had laid out their stakes in restaurant proximity to each other. 'They're sitting here,' Nigel muttered, 'so they can read the labels of their neighbour's wine bottles.'

'What's bothering this misanthrope?' I asked jokingly, addressing the question midway between father and son.

'It offends Nigel's socialist principles,' replied Holbrook. 'Nigel is probably the only person who's here because of Monteverdi and in spite of Glyndebourne.'

'Well, just look at this,' growled the son, pointing to a table that might well have been set by a butler. 'A *silver* vase with a *yellow* rose! And four *cut* crystal glasses! And *bone china* crockery! And a pepper *mill*! Can you imagine a picnic with an *ordinary* pepper shaker?' The sarcastic emphasis fell like beats of a drum.

'That will do, Nigel,' said Holbrook, who had been listening with a bemused smile. It was a warning, not an admonition; at that moment, a tall woman in silver brocade approached the table to rearrange the cutlery. She lifted the second knife at each setting and now placed it in a daring diagonal across the side plate, the tip pointing towards the chair. 'Felicity,' said a majestic man in evening clothes who was setting down a hamper, 'I'll take the caviar out of the cooler. It should be just right at intermission.'

'Christ!' growled Nigel. 'Let's go in. I can't take any more of this.'

At Glyndebourne music yields to gastronomy for the seventy-five minute dinner intermission – one reason why performances start so early. On dry English summer evenings, these formal picnics in the gardens are marvels of sartorial and social decorum. On the more common rainy days, the optimists – the people who had refused to take the precaution of advance bookings at one of the three restaurants on the grounds – withdraw to their automobiles. Then the Daimlers and big Rolls Royces become dining-rooms, the Jaguar sports cars and Porsches turn into dinettes.

Francis Holbrook didn't think I should gamble on English weather on my first visit to Glyndebourne. Like other cautious diners, he had ordered the entire four-course meal and wines a week in advance. The food was first-rate, the service irreproachable and timed in such a way that even the coffee could be drunk without undue haste before the first warning bell sounded. Nigel, however, excused himself after the *gravlax*, before the boned stuffed quail had even been served. 'I hope you don't mind,' he announced, 'but I'd like to go out into the garden.'

Holbrook raised his eyebrows. 'The garden? How will you bear the grinding of the pepper mills or the clinking of the glasses?'

'I'll manage,' muttered Nigel, and left.

'My son has become one kind of snob that you find only in our country,' chuckled my host. 'He joins the hunt and rides with the hounds, but he wants the fox to win.'

Nigel slipped into his seat just as the lights were dimmed for the second act of *Ulisse*. Afterwards, in the Bentley, Holbrook remarked, 'I say, Nigel, you're suddenly in a very jolly mood. Rather different from how you started out.'

His son ignored the comment. 'Thanks for taking me along, Father,' he said. 'It was quite a performance.'

'Even the garden scene? Did you become a Tory during intermission? If so, you ought to come back again.'

'I might,' replied Nigel.

Four days later, to my surprise I received from Nigel a second invitation to Glyndebourne: to *L'Italiana in Algeri*. 'We'll pick you up shortly after two; but I must warn you, if the weather is bad, we'll have to postpone it.'

In addition to Nigel, 'we' turned out to be a young couple in formal evening clothes and the uniformed chauffeur, who was Nigel's age. He was certainly not the man who last week had driven us in the Bentley, but the face looked familiar. It was Cedric, I realized, who had been at the guest seminar that I had given at Cambridge. He had virtually baited me at my talk, which had dealt with entrepreneurship in California's Silicon Valley; 'I rather think that we could do without lessons in free-market buccaneering' had been his last snide remark.

'Let me apologize for this mysterious invitation.' Nigel was sitting next to Cedric, who was driving the Mercedes estate wagon; now he turned to face me. 'I wasn't sure you'd accept if I told you about our plan.'

'You know how much I enjoyed our last trip to Glyndebourne. And I like youngish company.' The moment I had said 'youngish,' I realized how affected it sounded. 'Even if I wanted to, I couldn't change my mind now, at the speed we're travelling.'

Nigel didn't smile. 'The garden scene at Glyndebourne is a shameful spectacle – the number of people in Britain on the dole is going through the roof; all those millions starving in Africa; and these characters in black tie …'

'And the evening dresses,' inserted Pippa Stanley-Hunter, the bosomy brunette on my right, wearing a spectacularly décolleté gown. 'All of them act as if nothing had changed in the last fifty years.'

'Come off it, Nigel,' I said, 'Glyndebourne isn't all that bad. Besides, Africans don't like caviar.'

'Very funny,' replied Nigel.

I glanced at Pippa, but her pained expression made her loyalties clear. 'Go on,' I said, in no mood for dialectics.

Nigel hesitated, then bribed me with a smile. 'This isn't the place for socio-political discussions. Besides, both you and Dad are hopeless. We invited you because we needed somebody respectable looking and not too young.'

'Thanks,' I said, wryly.

'Just a statement of fact,' added Pippa.

'Did you notice the four hampers behind you?' asked Nigel.

'Yes. I was curious why we'd need four huge baskets for one opera intermission. You could feed dozens of starving …'

'Derek, why don't you open them?' Nigel's interruption ended my attempts at social commentary. I was getting curious: what did they really want from me?

The young man on my right turned around and lifted the cover of the container nearest him. It was empty.

'There's nothing in it,' I exclaimed.

'Right. Now open the next one,' ordered Nigel.

Derek reached farther back and flipped open the top of the second hamper, revealing stacked cans of Coca-Cola.

'Go on, Derek. Show him the fish and chips.'

'For heaven's sake, Nigel,' I said. 'So we're going to do penance for the culinary excesses of all the other people at Glyndebourne? You've got enough cokes for all of us and then some!'

It turned out that there was only one opera ticket – even that had been difficult to get – but a flash of the envelope was enough to get us past the attendant into the car park. Cedric, in chauffeur's livery, was ignored completely as he carried one of the hampers to the spot Nigel had selected the week before. On one side we were sheltered by a hedge, yet we were within easy sight and hearing of the oval picnic area that was so popular. While Nigel walked with me through the gardens – so we would be seen together by as many people as possible – the others removed the blanket from the hamper and arranged the four picnic settings. When we returned, Derek was sitting on the blanket, his elbow on the closed hamper, surveying the scene. Pippa was sipping wine. Nobody would've guessed that the wine was a cheap Bulgarian Cabernet Sauvignon, the current 'in' drink at Cambridge, or that under the debonair aloofness of this handsome couple seethed thoughts of crushing unemployment in Liverpool and bloated bellies in the Sudan.

'Let's go,' announced Nigel. 'When we get to the tennis court, you turn left toward the auditorium with the rest of the crowd, while we head for the car. We'll wait there until the performance has started. Cedric will take the next hamper out and fiddle around like somebody's chauffeur till he's sure everyone is inside, and then he'll get us. We'll fetch the other hampers. Between us we ought to finish everything in just a few minutes.'

I was amazed how cool they were. But why not? They fitted so perfectly into the Glyndebourne milieu – dress, accent, bearing; no wonder British spies like Guy Burgess remained undetected for so long. But what about me? Did I look as conspicuous as I felt? I didn't remember ever having worn a tuxedo in the middle of the afternoon, and here I was in a rented one for the second time in a week. I wasn't even certain of my role. Witness? Co-conspirator? Or just a prop? We were practically at the tennis court when Nigel turned to me, for the first time sounding anxious.

'You've got an aisle seat. *Please* leave the moment the curtain falls and hurry to our picnic site. Start taking out some of the food from the hamper – at least the smoked salmon – and put it on the plates. We'll come as soon as the rest of the crowd moves across the lawns. Thanks and good luck.'

Good luck? I mused. Had I just been promoted? But so far I hadn't done anything and I didn't intend to. People would see me inside at the opera – there'd be no way that I could be implicated, I hoped. Still, I had agreed to go along.

I wasn't the only one to skip the first act curtain call of Elvira, Isabella and Mustafa. Some members of the Glyndebourne audience always duck out before the lights go on – delegated by friends, wives or parents to run to the car for the missing delicacies, or to open the wine bottles so that the claret has some chance to breathe. Still, I was one of the first at our section of the garden and like a veteran Glyndebourner I opened our hamper, the one that Derek had not shown me in the car. Now I understood the reason:

the thinly cut, pale pink, smoked salmon most certainly didn't come from a proletarian grocery store, nor did the Strasbourg goose liver pâté with truffles. I had barely arranged the salmon slices on the plates when Nigel and his two friends arrived.

'Toss the salad, darling,' said Derek as he handed the long fork and spoon to Pippa. 'I'll handle the wine.'

'Where is Cedric?' I asked. 'What's he eating?'

'Fish and chips,' grinned Nigel. 'Surely, we can't have the chauffeur eat here.'

'I've only had time to take out the smoked salmon and the pâté,' I said.

'I hope you noticed it had truffles,' interrupted Derek. 'I robbed the family pantry.'

'So I did. And I haven't even opened some of the other packages. But I did see the Fortnum & Mason labels, you parlour socialists.'

Nigel tapped me gently on the hand with the long baguette which he was in the process of breaking into four pieces. 'Don't touch them yet,' he grinned. 'They're for later. Just trifles, so to speak.'

'I presume we're all eating this for the sake of authenticity rather than socialist principles.' One of my habits is to hide discomfort behind banter.

'Precisely,' replied Nigel.

'Oh, look! Quick! There it starts,' Pippa whispered. 'The table just to the right of the woman in green. I knew this was going to be a good lark.'

I didn't have the faintest idea which dinner groups they had picked, but I should have realized that the smallish oval would be a prime target, since the diners at their tables or on the blankets were so close together. Perhaps it was my unconscious guilt that had made me sit with my back towards that area: if I couldn't see those people, they couldn't see me ...

Pippa went on, *pianissimo*. 'They're the ones with the Beaujolais. I figured anybody cheap enough to drink that stuff might as well get the Coca-Cola. Look how he's talking to his wife; she's got to be his wife, otherwise she wouldn't pretend nothing was wrong.' She leaned forward to stifle her laughter. 'Look how she's pouring! As if it were exactly what they'd intended to have all along: coke in cut crystal! I might as well tell you,' she dropped her voice even further, 'their Beaujolais went to the couple sitting on the blanket just below the bloke looking at his coke. I exchanged it for their Château Talbot, which is now back with Cedric in the car. Nigel, I can't keep staring at them; but do tell me when they realize it.'

The excitement of my companions was infectious; I almost felt like a participant. 'Let's see,' said Nigel, who had put on mirrored glasses in spite of the fact that the sun had already set. He seemed to have thought of everything. I hate those glasses, where you can't see the other person's eyes; instead you catch your own distorted image in miniature. But they were ideal for his purpose. 'He's opening one of the bottles. It's wrapped in a napkin ...'

'I did that!' Pippa expressed her triumph *sotto voce*. 'I figured he'd miss the Beaujolais label.'

'Splendid!' Nigel's two blank mirrors pointed in the direction of the impending disaster. 'He's pouring some in his glass ... he's lifting it ... it's at his lips ...' Nigel raised his own glass to act out his patter.

'Somebody tell me what's going on,' I demanded.

Nigel motioned with his hand; a muffled 'wait!' keeping me in suspense. 'He's unfolding the napkin ...'

Even with my back toward the scene, I could hear

the bellowed 'Bloody awful Beaujolais! Who in blazes brought this stuff?' I had to turn around. What I saw was a farcical tableau by Feydeau: the outraged Beaujolais taster on the blanket – his Château-Talbot palate violated; the ex-Beaujolais owner sitting just above him, a wine glass full of Coca-Cola in his hand, the slow recognition of infamy spilling over his face; and the rest of the crowd – the men in black, the women competing in colour with the flowers – startled by decibel levels usually heard only inside the auditorium, not in this most English of English garden settings.

'Nigel,' broke in Pippa, 'which table did you favour with the fish and chips?'

'None here. I took that hamper to the other side of the hedge.' He rose from the blanket. 'This general had better inspect that battlefield.'

'I say, those four over there do have style.' Derek was pouring himself some more of the Bulgarian wine. Now he pointed behind me. 'They had a top notch basket: a big tin of real Beluga caviar and the best wine of the lot. The two bottles of the '76 Latour will bring us at least two hundred quid at the auction ...'

'Auction?' I had barely adjusted to my status as an innocent participant in a risky escapade, when the ante was again being raised. 'What auction?'

I didn't like the complacency in his face. 'You think it rather beastly of us not to have told you earlier, don't you? I hope you didn't think we were thieves. We're the modern Robin Hoods of Glyndebourne: we're organizing a fancy-food auction at Cambridge ...'

'Derek, let me guess,' I interrupted. 'With the proceeds from the caviar and the wines and all the other loot you'll buy corn and wheat for Africa.'

Derek raised his glass and winked. 'What I left them instead was the cheapest Chianti we could find and some of those bright red salmon eggs – a huge glass jar. They can't miss it. But look at them. I thought they'd be bloody angry, but they seem to be having an outrageous time. The man with the waxed moustache has been pouring the wine as if it were the best claret in the world – he's even wrapped a napkin around it. And *he* did it,' Derek was addressing Pippa, 'not I. I wanted to be damn sure he would see the Chianti label, although the shape of the bottle alone would've told him this was no Château Latour. Look how she's laughing with that big spoon full of red goo. If they're snobs, at least they've got a sense of humour. Or maybe they're actors!'

From the distance, I saw Nigel approaching. He seemed disappointed. There was nothing Robin-Hoodish in his demeanour. After sitting down, he started to play with the trifle in his dish, which we had filled during his absence.

'What's the report from the fish and chips front?' When Nigel didn't reply, Pippa prompted once more. 'Well?'

He shrugged his shoulders. 'I'll tell you later.'

I was getting a bit tired of the joke, although I'd been laughing along with the three of them. It was time to stretch my legs before the start of the second act. 'We'll wait for you in the car,' called Nigel as I headed for the formal flower garden.

The first burst of applause following the final septet had just broken out. I was waiting for Frederica von Stade to make her curtain call; she'd sung a superb Isabella, and the spaghetti scene had been greeted by the audience with uproarious laughter. I stayed until the very last *brava*. As I pushed my way through the crowd, I saw Nigel waving at me.

'You didn't have to come for me,' I said. 'I remember where the car was parked.'

'That's not why I'm here,' he replied a bit sheepishly. 'We have another passenger in the car. Please don't bring up our prank with the food.'

'How did you end up with another passenger?' I asked.

'Wait 'til we get out,' said Nigel as he led the way towards the tennis courts.

'I still can't fathom how our hamper had fish and chips and those Cox's Orange Pippin apples,' said Millicent. I never did hear her last name when we exchanged introductions in the car, nor did I catch a good look at the young woman as I climbed into the Mercedes. All I got were flash exposures of her left profile – the curly dark hair, pudgy nose and slightly protruding teeth – from the occasional headlights of oncoming traffic. This time, Derek was driving, Nigel in the seat next to him, the two women and I in the back seat, and Cedric stretched out behind us among the four food baskets. 'And it came from Harrod's,' she added in a plaintive voice.

'Did you see them pack the basket?' asked Pippa.

'No. I called Harrod's from the office. Mr Shaw only invited me the day before, when a Japanese client of the firm cancelled his trip.'

'Was Shaw the grim man sitting at your table and staring at the crowd?' asked Nigel.

'He was bloody angry when he opened the brand new wicker basket. I also got it at Harrod's – I believe it's called The Glyndebourner.'

A muffled 'You don't say!' could be heard from the front.

'I guess Mr Shaw wasn't talking to me anymore when you saw us.' It was clear that Millicent hadn't caught the sarcasm in Nigel's voice. 'He's a bit stiff in the office, but he's a fair boss, and you can't really blame him. I didn't believe it at first when he told me I could pay up to a couple of hundred quid for the hamper and food. Mr Shaw isn't usually much of a spendthrift. But then he explained all about Glyndebourne and how his Japanese guest would never forget it …'

'Still, it was pretty mean to blame you,' said Pippa. 'Harrod's obviously made a mistake when they filled your order.'

'I can't imagine Harrod's carrying fish and chips. You should've heard the food consultant they put on the phone when I explained I was ordering a basket for Glyndebourne and wanted some advice. I've never eaten quail eggs in aspic; I don't even know what the dish looks like. And the caviar – I don't believe you can guess what a small tin costs. Or maybe you can; you've probably drunk the champagne they recommended. Moët,' she added, putting the emphasis on the first syllable. 'I can still hear the way the gentleman from Harrod's described the sweets: "profiteroles stuffed with heavy pastry cream and smothered with ripe strawberries".'

'Well, maybe somebody in the shipping department did it for a lark.'

'For a lark?' Millicent sounded indignant.

'Maybe it wasn't a lark,' interjected Nigel. 'Perhaps it was a protest.'

'Against what?'

'Why, against all the waste and ostentatiousness of

these Glyndebourne intermission feasts.'

'I rather fancied it and I didn't see much waste. And what did you people eat?'

I decided it was time to come to Nigel's rescue. I owed it to him for *L'Italiana*. 'How come you ended up with us here in the car? What happened to your Mr Shaw?'

Nigel took over immediately. 'The prig abandoned her! When I came by the second time, after all the people had left for the next act, I saw Millicent alone; she was sobbing. I told her we didn't have tickets and were just accompanying you to the opera. I felt she might as well return with a more sympathetic crowd than that grouch Shaw.'

'It's such a shame. This was my first opera and I don't even know how it ended.' So far Millicent had ignored me completely, but now she addressed me. 'You saw it all. What happened in the second act?'

'It ends with one of the funniest scenes in opera,' I started, without thinking. 'You remember in the first act how Mustafa, the Bey of Algiers, falls in love with his Italian captive, Isabella, who in turn is in love with the Bey's slave, Livorno?'

'Lovely, wasn't it?' she nodded.

'Well, in the second act, Isabella dupes Mustafa by cooking a huge dish of spaghetti with tomato sauce and cheese. She grates the Parmesan while singing in full voice, and then escapes with her lover because Mustafa is totally preoccupied with the first spaghetti he has ever seen.'

'God, I'm hungry,' she sighed. 'I could even eat fish and chips. I didn't have any lunch – I was saving myself.' She gave a hollow laugh.

'Crawl back here with me,' said Cedric. 'We've got plenty of food left. You'll have to take pot-luck, though; it's dark back here.' His last words hung tumescently in the silent car.

Cedric had hardly finished with his invitation; he was still pushing the baskets around to create additional room while Millicent was already clambering over the back seat. 'Come, sit over here,' murmured Cedric. 'I'll open the basket and you just reach in.'

After some giggling, we heard Millicent's disappointed voice. 'Stilton! It's the one cheese I don't fancy.'

'Never mind, there's lot's of stuff here. Let me see what I find. Try this,' he said after a pause. 'It's soft and it doesn't smell of cheese. In fact, I can't smell anything through the paper. Better use a spoon.'

I could hear the rustle of paper and the subsequent purr of delight. 'Ah, this is better, much better. Cedric, take a bite and tell me what you think it is.'

'Squishy eggs,' he said laughingly, his mouth still full.

'You're right,' she exclaimed. 'But what kind?'

'Maybe it says on the wrapper,' suggested Cedric.

I could see Nigel's instinctive gesture, but it was too late for any warning. Millicent had flipped on the inside-light switch.

'Why ...' she commenced and then stopped abruptly. I had turned around just in time to see her rummage through the other packages. 'You bloody bastards,' she screeched. 'So *you* did it!' And with that cry the bombardment started.

The first missile, the quail eggs nested in aspic, hit Nigel on the shoulder. The next one, the profiteroles, shot past me to splatter against the inside windshield.

'For Christ's sake, stop it,' exclaimed Derek as he slammed on the brakes. 'I can't see.' But it was too late.

He swerved onto the shoulder of the road and sideswiped a post bearing an RAC emergency telephone. I was thrown against the back of Nigel's seat. He and Derek jumped out of the car and raced around to open the back of the estate wagon. But the interval was sufficient for the enraged Millicent to empty the remainder of her dinner basket all over the car. I only saw the cover of Harrod's special Mango Chutney being ripped off and the contents poured over Pippa's back and bare shoulders. As she lurched forward, the mess moved down between her breasts like lava.

Millicent climbed out of the back, her hands dripping, the front of her dress like a painter's pallet. 'You poncey little Cambridge shits,' she shouted, tearful, and stalked off towards the distant lights of a petrol station.

I was the last one out. My head was starting to ache and as I touched my forehead, I felt a sticky ooze. Cautiously I got out of the car and approached Nigel, whose starched white shirt looked blood-spattered from the strawberries. He pointed at the smashed front grill and the huge dent in the left fender.

'Christ,' he muttered. 'How am I going to explain that one to my father?'

'Nigel,' I said, 'could you help me? I think I'm bleeding.'

He glanced at me quickly and then leaned forward, his eyes narrowing, as if he wanted to get me into sharper focus.

'You'll be OK,' he said, and started to rummage in his pockets. I thought that he was searching for a handkerchief to wipe off the blood which had started to run into my eyes. Instead he produced a comb, made of tortoise shell with silver trimming on top and one side. 'Here, comb the caviar out of your hair.'

THE PSOMOPHILE

Even before you heard him speak, it was evident that he was not an American. There were traces of Spanish (*'espectacular'* he would say) and on occasion Italian touches, superimposed on Briticisms of the 'jolly-bloody-beastly' variety; a good guess might have been an Italian family in South America, say Argentina or Uruguay, who had sent their son to an English school. He wore only custom-made English shoes. His jackets were invariably of Italian design and tight, though not too tight; double-breasted; and made of materials such as Venetian wool, which didn't lose its press even in rain, or checkered cashmere. He now lived in Hillsborough, one of the wealthiest suburbs of San Francisco, and commuted to the city in a chauffeur-driven Jaguar.

But his real mark was his passion for bread. Not all baked goods, and certainly not cakes, but bread – or rolls. Once a friend called him a *paniphile* but he could not accept a bastardized Greco-Latin term. After some debate, they telephoned a Cypriot acquaintance, who narrowed their choices to two. *Artophile* was probably the more correct, based on the ancient Greek *artos* for loaf, but the potential for confusion was bothersome. Of course he was an art lover – one only had to see the walls of his home or office – but ambiguity simply would not do when dealing with bread, and the word *artophile* would sound like another hybrid. *Psomophile* also seemed flawed since the ancient Greeks used *psomos* for a scrap of bread or meat, but their Cypriot, insisting that '*psomi* is the modern Greek for bread', hung up. The word was accepted by the psomophile, who noted that suffering from *psomophilia* sounded deliciously degenerate.

One clear autumn Saturday in 1980, the psomophile turned incipient psomomaniac. The man and his wife had been invited to brunch at the home of a Berkeley professor. They arrived late – a Latin habit. Their host led them straight to the buffet table, suggesting that they help themselves before meeting the other visitors. As the hostess brought in a basket, this firm believer in edible art noticed that the food was already in disarray, but for once he did not mind the violations committed by the earlier guests: the excised truffles from the pâté, the cucumber slice dropped into the hummus or even the crushed curls of the butter aliquots. His nostrils had started to quiver, the way a man's might when he discerns a perfume on a woman. At first sight, the warm round loaf carried by the hostess might have looked like ordinary hard-crusted, sourdough bread. But to his eyes the imperfections of the bread's surface – the manner in which the edges of the multiple knife slashes tended to sear, or the size of the subcutaneous bubbles of the crust – were unmistakable evidence of a special touch.

There was a component in the aroma that he could not place, that made him salivate. As soon as the hostess had deposited the basket on the table, he headed for it with a serrated breadknife to perform the inevitable ritual: to cut the end piece of the loaf, because it offered the maximum amount of crust, the real proof of a baker's art, and yet enough flesh to permit insight into the body of the bread. The moment that he tasted it, he knew. It was Parmesan! Just the slightest trace, but divine! He glanced around and furtively cut the other end of the loaf. He did not notice what other food he had picked; it was all camouflage for the bread.

Out on the deck he complimented the hostess on her omelette, which he had not yet tasted, and on the bread. 'How did you get the idea for the Parmesan taste? So subtle and yet a real signature! Who taught you how to bake such a masterpiece?'

'You're the first to recognize the Parmesan. But I can't take credit for it, I got it from Alessandro's.'

'Alessandro's?'

'They're a local bakery, third-generation Italian, who somehow combine San Franciso sourdough with Italian baking. It's only on Saturdays that they bake this bread.'

He had little difficulty following her directions to Alessandro's. The display window looked as if it had not been washed for days; and except for a few lonely items – a tray containing some rolls, a cake or two – it was empty. But to the seasoned psomophile, the bakery looked promising. It was obvious that most goods had been sold and that displaymanship was either scorned by the owner or unnecessary.

A tinny bell rang as he opened the door. After an insolent interval, an elderly man in coat and tie appeared through the rear door. 'Yes?' was all he said. The psomophile's request for a loaf of Saturday's special bread produced a snort. 'At one thirty?' the baker asked, pointing to the clock on the wall. 'We're always sold out by ten fifteen. We open at ten.'

Next Saturday morning at nine forty a uniformed chauffeur in the psomophile's racing-green Jaguar was parked in front of Alessandro's bakery, reading a newspaper. The display window was fuller than last week but still had not been washed. As the first customers appeared in front of the closed door, the chauffeur folded his paper and joined the line. Promptly at ten, the door was unlocked. With hardly an exception, the requests were for 'the Special'. When the chauffeur ordered five loaves, he was told, 'Two to a customer, unless you order ahead of time.'

During the next few weeks the chauffeur became a familiar Saturday figure at the bakery. One morning the chauffeur was accompanied by his employer, who made a simple request. 'Hold three loaves for me every Saturday, even if the chauffeur is not here by ten. If I want more, I'll order ahead of time.' The baker understood a compliment, even when it was disguised as an order; and especially when the order for a month's supply was paid without even requesting a receipt. In return, Alessandro volunteered a piece of information: if frozen promptly, his loaves could be preserved for years, not weeks or months, and would still taste like fresh bread, provided – the right index finger was raised for emphasis – each loaf was defrosted slowly while wrapped tightly in a moist towel. 'Slowly,' he repeated, his finger jabbing at the cashmere jacket just below the silk handkerchief, 'and never heat the bread until it's completely defrosted. And don't re-freeze it.'

For the next couple of years, Alessandro's Saturday Special could always be found in the kitchen of the Hillsborough home. Usually the psomophile consumed one of the fresh loaves within a few hours of the bread's arrival in his kitchen. The rest was cut into half-loaves, each section wrapped tightly in plastic, and frozen. Defrosting by the moist-towel technique worked as promised, but he never tested the 'for years' guarantee.

One Saturday, in late 1982, the chauffeur returned with three loaves and the news that Alessandro's bakery would be closed forever. The reasons were mysterious – some of the customers claimed it was loss of the lease, others alluded to a sudden rupture between the elder Alessandro and his son. Whatever the cause, next Saturday was going to be the last day when Alessandro's Special could be purchased.

The psomophile learned from Alessandro over the phone that money was not the problem, that the decision was irrevocable, but that the baker was prepared for a grand gesture, though not the grandest of them all: divulging the recipe for the bread. This was out of the question; he was not even willing to disclose the origin of the Parmesan, except for warning that only one imported brand would do. However, he would accept a special order for one hundred loaves of his bread to be fetched on the last day of his bakery's existence. Alessandro asked only that the Jaguar park in the back alley and not show up until noon. He expected a lot of his regular customers that morning; relinquishing one hundred loaves in front of them would permanently tarnish his reputation for tough even-handedness.

The Jaguar arrived in the alley at eleven fifty. The psomophile wore a dark blue suit with blue and black striped tie, his version of a mourning suit. Alessandro opened the door the moment the chauffeur and his passenger approached the bakery's rear entrance. Twenty or more white paper bags were stacked against the wall. 'You've only got ninety-five loaves here.' He had sold out earlier than usual and a couple of his oldest customers were so disappointed that he just didn't have the heart to send them away. 'I hope you don't mind. Not that you could do anything about it,' he smiled wryly, still calling the shots. The Jaguar's boot could not cope with all the bread; the overflow rode inside the car and filled it with a strange aroma of Parmesan, British leather and freshly baked bread.

The chauffeur, the cook, the maid, and the master of the house set to work cutting all but five loaves into three parts, and wrapping each portion tightly in plastic. The five whole loaves were left uncut for a few special events. Only when the bread was ready to be frozen did it dawn on them that 275 parcels, five of them rather bulky ones, would usurp the entire freezer capacity of the kitchen. Without a moment's hesitation the order was issued to remove the current contents of the freezer – pound after pound of steaks, sausages, fish, sweet butter, ice cream, and various unlabelled containers, all dear to the cook. She promptly went to bed, not to reappear until Monday morning.

The psomophile decided to be selfish. With very few exceptions, this bread was to be consumed only by him and his wife, and even they would restrict themselves to one frozen portion per week. Given his frequent travels, the supply was likely to last for at least six years. He refused to worry beyond that time.

February of 1986 was the wettest month in eighty years of San Francisco weather records. The torrential rains, spawned by a series of Pacific storms, were accompanied by very high gusts, causing power failures of unprecedented length. San Francisco was relatively unscathed, especially the downtown office and hotel areas; most of the occupants of these high-rise buildings were unaware of what was happening just a few miles north, south, and east of the city, where power transmission was largely above ground. Shortly after lunch, the man's secretary interrupted him at a meeting. The note which she presented discreetly referred to a message from his wife, reporting that the electricity in their home had been interrupted since ten in the morning; their dinner was likely to be a cold buffet. 'Reserve a suite at the Huntington,' he said, 'and tell my wife we'll spend the night in the city.' Dinner without guests in the city, perhaps followed by a visit to a cinema, was a luxury that both relished but only rarely indulged.

The morning did not start propitiously. Not only did he have to dress in the same clothes that he had worn the day before, but a dollop of marmalade had landed on his tie to produce the type of sartorial blemish that he would never have tolerated under ordinary circumstances. And then the telephone rang. The maid was calling from Hillsborough to say that the electric service had still not been restored. What were she and the cook to do about the thawing food in the freezer?

'Oh, forget about it,' he said, but before his wife could pass this on, the enormity of the maid's message sank in: the bread, a minimum of three-years' worth of Alessandro's Special. A glance at his pocket diary told him he could head south by eleven a.m. Perhaps the insulation of the freezer was such that the bread was still frozen; perhaps the electricity would come on earlier than expected.

The situation was even more serious than he had

imagined. On the car radio he learned that crews were coming from as far away as Nevada to help in the repair work; no estimate could be given about the timing of the restoration of electric service. As the chauffeur drove through one of the poorest sections of town on the way to the freeway, past flophouses, run-down hotels, boarded-up buildings, and figures huddled in doorways attempting to keep dry, the psomophile thought morosely about the rapidly thawing, if not totally unfrozen, three years' supply of irreplaceable bread. The prospect of a bread-eating orgy did not console him – where was he going to find forty or fifty guests who'd want to eat bread and cheese in this rain, in a dark, cold house? The Jaguar was idling at a traffic light when he saw a line of impoverished men and women pressed against the wall of a building, waiting for the door to open for the free lunch at the San Francisco Gospel Mission.

The rain had stopped in the early afternoon, but a strong wind was still blowing. The latest guesstimate was that electric service would not be restored until midnight at the earliest. The chauffeur and the maid loaded the bread into the trunk of the Jaguar. They had not bothered wrapping 150 odd sections in wet towels – the bread was virtually defrosted before they even departed; it was certain that it would be completely edible by the time they reached the Mission.

The chauffeur was strangely silent as his passenger alluded to Christ and His miracle of the loaves; he couldn't even force a laugh in response to his employer's boast that Alessandro's bread probably tasted better than His. So enamoured had the psomophile become of the biblical analogy that he had not given any thought to the impression that his arrival in a Jaguar, chauffeur-driven, would make on Skid Row. The driver, however, had been thinking of nothing else. His worst fears were realized the moment their car pulled up at the converted store front and he saw the dull surprise, mixed with hostility, in the eyes of the people waiting for the opening of the dining-room. In addition to the soup-kitchen clientele, there were loiterers all down the block. A large proportion of these were black and more gregarious than the people in the waiting line. Many were smoking; two big black men were drinking beer. All stared, and some laughed, as the tall man in the camel-hair coat and the uniformed chauffeur loaded themselves with several white paper parcels each. The men headed through the crowd for the front door, where they found themselves blocked by a nearly toothless old man in dilapidated clothing. 'They ain't open until five,' he said without moving. The chauffeur looked grimly at his employer, whose sudden helplessness seemed so totally out of character.

'Excuse me, please,' mumbled the psomophile as he tried to slide past the old man to the door, only to realize that with his hands full of bread, his feet were the sole available doorknocker. A few genteel taps produced no response. Losing all patience, the chauffeur pushed past the old man and repeatedly kicked the door until a thin youth, in blue jeans and grey smock, opened it a crack. 'What the hell ...' he started, but then stopped abruptly as two bags were thrust at him.

'Take these and let us in.' The commanding sharpness of these words sufficed for the men's admittance, whereupon the door was slammed before the pushing crowd could follow.

By the time the donation was approved by the kitchen manager and the first load of parcels opened, the chauffeur was perspiring heavily; even his employer showed beads of moisture on his forehead. As they left the dining-room for a second load, accompanied by the young man who had opened the door, they found a scene from a post-war movie.

The two black men with their beer were relaxing on the sloping bonnet of the Jaguar as if on a park bench. Others were leaning against the windows and doors of the car – a human collage on green. Four people, one a spaced-out woman in a torn red ski jacket and purplish woollen cap, were lounging on the boot of the automobile – its rear window serving as the woman's pillow. The chauffeur didn't even have time to pounce on these exterior passengers. A wave of the young man's hand scattered the motley crew, whereupon the psomophile slid into the car and quickly locked the door.

The chauffeur and shelter attendant moved a second load of bread into the Gospel Mission. They were about to assemble a third batch when the shelter door was unlocked. Immediately, the crowd around the Jaguar thinned as the waiting line of men and women pushed their way into the dining-room. Only the two beer drinkers and a few smokers, apparently not regular customers of the soup kitchen, remained around the car. For the first time, the automobile's occupant felt some relief. All he wished now was for the driver's reappearance so that they could depart from this most un-Galilean environment. However, the person bursting out of the dining-room was not the chauffeur. The old man, who had initially blocked their way, began to bang his fist on the window of the car. As the psomophile looked at him astonished, he spotted the blood trickling out of the old man's open mouth. He recognized, between the man's thumb and index finger, a tooth. Only then did the rush of obscenities reaching him through the protective Jaguar shell make sense: the old man had broken it on the hard crust of Alessandro's Special – probably a bit harder than usual since it had not been defrosted according to the rules, but not too hard for the teeth of a Hillsborough resident who visits the dentist twice a year. Suddenly he realized that what he adored in this bread – the hardy crust, the unusual taste and aroma – might, to the uninitiated brought up on soft white cardboard, suggest spoilage.

The old man threw his tooth at the window, producing a minute and yet distinctly angry-sounding ping against the glass, and rushed back into the dining-room. The two beer drinkers on the Jaguar's bonnet had stopped laughing. For the first time, they showed some interest in one of the soup kitchen's clients. The dining-room door broke open again. A small mob, led by the old man with a piece of Alessandro's bread in each hand, stormed towards the car and began to pelt it with bread missiles, the thumps reverberating down the block. The beer drinkers jumped off the bonnet, leaving their beer cans still resting on it. The woman in the red ski jacket raised one of the intact loaves, and threw it at the door, causing the man inside to duck instinctively. By now, the beer drinkers had decided to make a sport of the debacle. One of the men picked up the round loaf from the gutter and threw it to his companion, who had resumed his seat on the bonnet as the initial bombardment had slowed down due to lack of ammunition. Laughing, the two men passed their bread ball back and forth, back and forth.

The scene lasted only a minute or two. Just as the

first wave of assault started its retreat to the dining-room, the chauffeur pushed his way through the crowd, quickly unlocked the car, and started the motor. He blew his horn several times but the commanding sound made no impression on the ball player on the bonnet. Placing the bread loaf between his legs, he leaned forward to face the chauffeur through the windshield. 'Drive on, James,' he said, but it was unlikely that the driver heard. What he did catch was an angry growl from the back seat, 'Damn you, Lester, get moving.' It was the first time in their eleven years together that the man had cursed his chauffeur.

As the Jaguar crept out of its parking place, the black man on its bonnet let out a whoop of delight as he raised his bread trophy into the air. Dozens of pedestrians turned; a passing school-bus of children screamed with pleasure at the sight. Within fifty yards, the Jaguar came to a stop at a red light, and the human bonnet ornament jumped off the car. With an elegant, dismissive gesture, he threw the loaf high into the air. It made a loud thud as it hit the Jaguar's bonnet, before rolling into the centre of the Howard Street traffic. Before the eyes of the passenger and the chauffeur, the loaf was flattened by a passing truck.

The Jaguar shot forward the moment the light turned green. Only then did the passenger notice the bags of bread sitting next to the driver's seat, the ones that had never been taken into the soup kitchen. A sudden wave of nausea engulfed him; it was clear that he would never be able to touch the last precious crusts of Alessandro's bread. It was even conceivable that the psomophile would never want to eat bread again.

SLEIGHT-OF-MIND

One trick always left me baffled. He prompted you to select a card, made you shuffle the deck after you'd replaced the card, and then asked you – gently, an apologetic smile hidden in the typically Japanese manner by his hand over his mouth – to spread the cards, face down, all over the table surface. 'Now separate them into two piles,' he would say, with a motion of his hand over the scattered cards as if he were cutting a cake in half. After a moment's hesitation, he'd discard one of the piles and ask you to repeat the process until only two cards remained on the table. He'd point to one of them and without a further word, just a discreet gesture, dare you to turn it face up. Invariably, it was the card that you'd selected originally.

Professor Jiko Nishinaka was an internationally known biochemical entomologist accustomed to showing off in front of huge audiences. He was a consummate performer – as a scientific lecturer as well as an amateur magician. 'Amateur' was hardly the correct term: he didn't charge for his performances, but they were supremely skilled. His magician's repertoire covered everything from simple sleight-of-hand tricks – coins out of ears, vanishing handkerchiefs, all but the proverbial live rabbit – to phenomenal manipulations with cards.

This occasion, however, was no ordinary lecture. The audience was small: seven persons, all men, who had gathered for coffee and dessert after listening to Nishinaka give the annual Bowman lecture. Nishinaka was just warming up. He shuffled the deck with a speed and clatter that would have done honour to a blackjack dealer in Las Vegas.

'Quick! Pick one and don't intellectualize. Now put it back,' he said, without taking his eyes off our host. Nishinaka quickly arranged the cards in a giant fan.

'Keep thinking of the card you picked,' he reminded our host as he fingered one card after another. Suddenly he stopped, a card between his thumb and index finger.

'It was a spade, wasn't it?' To me, it seemed more of a judgement, but our host took it as a question. He nodded.

'Then it's this one,' said Nishinaka, flipping the two of spades onto the table. He accepted the exclamation, 'That's it!' with a modest shrug: 'All you need is practice.'

The reaction of the group was typical of academics, and especially of men who claim to be professional seekers of answers. Several explanations were bandied about – all of them in the third person, as if Nishinaka had become invisible.

'I bet he saw the card reflected in Gilbert's pupil. Didn't you see how he was staring at him?'

'Maybe the cards are marked in some way – after all, they're his cards.'

'It could've been a fingerprint. Did you notice how he examined each card after shuffling?'

I was grinning like an impresario – after all, I'd nominated Nishinaka for this year's Bowman lecture – when I realized that one man had remained silent:

our Nobel laureate, the neurobiologist. He'd come to the Bowman because he chaired the selection committee for this prestigious affair, which includes a medal and a handsome honorarium. Furthermore, Nishinaka's topic, 'Sensory Perception and Communication among Invertebrates', interested him. But the reason that he'd stopped after dinner was pure and nasty curiosity. At the Bowman committee meeting, apropos of nothing, I'd brought up Nishinaka's phenomenal card tricks. Nishinaka would have winced if he'd heard me use the word 'tricks' – he considered the term demeaning – but then he wasn't present when I bragged about him.

'I suggest we invite Professor Nishinaka in spite of such non-scientific credentials,' our Nobelist had interjected, 'and then have a post-prandial examination by this committee of extrasensory perception among higher vertebrates.' He'd winked at me, but instead of winking back, I'd looked down. Suddenly, I'd gotten worried.

Our Nobelist was usually *primus inter pares* and this time he played the role to the hilt.

'Professor Nishinaka, that was quite clever,' he said with his dangerous lupine smile that I'd seen at many a scientific lecture. The speaker expected a compliment; instead it was a preamble to a question, innocent in tone but devastating in content. Looking at us rather than Nishinaka – as if he meant to say 'watch me take care of him' – he asked, 'Do you need to touch the cards?'

'No, I don't.'

'Do you have to be present when the card is selected?' he continued.

Nishinaka hesitated. He was accustomed to questions after his performances, but usually they were not cross-examinations. 'No, not really,' he replied, after a pause.

'You don't? Then what *do* you need to do?'

The answer came instantaneously. 'You've got to be willing to concentrate on the card while I look you in the eye; just think of the card rather than trying to figure out how I do it.'

There was a faint smile on the Nobelist's face as he turned to our host. 'Gilbert, do you have any cards in the house?'

Nishinaka flushed before our host could even respond. The implication behind the request was obvious, but he let it pass.

'Yes,' said our host. 'We may even have a new deck. I'll be back in a moment.'

The cards were still in their plastic wrapping. 'Thanks,' said the Nobel laureate as he stuffed the torn wrapper into the empty ash tray. 'And now, Professor Nishinaka, would you be good enough to excuse yourself?'

As soon as Nishinaka had left, the Nobel prize winner rose and went into a corner of the living-room. In plain sight of all of us, he carefully separated the deck by holding the cards at their edges with the tip of his fingers – the way someone might handle a stack of hot plates. It was clear that he intended to leave no fingerprints, nor was he letting any of us see which card he'd chosen. His shuffling was slow and clumsy. But there was no derision, no sound. We all understood that we were observing a scientist eliminate one more experimental variable: a moist fingerprint on the clear surface of the brand new card.

The Nobel laureate returned to his seat and placed the stacked cards on the table immediately in front of him. 'Would one of you please call the man?'

As I left the room, the laureate's voice – the contrast between his earlier 'Professor Nishinaka' and the contemptuous 'man' he'd just used – grated on me. I wanted to make it up to my friend. 'Jiko,' I remarked, patting his shoulder, 'they're ready for you. Good luck.'

'Thanks,' was all he said, his look an untroubled mask.

'Professor Nishinaka,' announced the Nobel laureate before I'd even closed the door, 'I'm the only one who has seen the card in this stack here on the table.' He motioned with his head towards the tightly packed deck. 'Which one did I pick?'

The question was asked with such uncharacteristic bluntness that I sensed an undercurrent of concern; as if he wanted to say, 'You aren't really going to try, are you? You can't possibly guess which card I chose, can you?'

I've always been impressed by the way some Japanese can assume uncomfortable positions and maintain them for what seem to me intolerable periods of time. Nishinaka, who was exceptionally tall for a Japanese, quickly squatted on his heels in order to face the Nobelist at eye level. He was so close that his adversary unconsciously drew back in his seat. There was a nervous silence as the rest of us grouped around the two men. They reminded me of wrestlers ready to spring. Nishinaka said nothing. He had fastened on the Nobelist's eyes like a magnet on an iron bar.

After a disconcertingly long silence Nishinaka slowly shook his head. 'It's not a numbered card,' he murmured as if he were talking to himself. 'No, it isn't. Am I right?' he asked somewhat louder, addressing his challenger.

'That's right,' was the curt reply.

The head shaking became more pronounced, the low monologue even more hesitating. 'I can't catch it, it's not the queen, it's not the king ... it's not a jack ... not the ace ... it's a black card ...'

The Nobelist's eyes had hardened, his lips were pressed together tightly; he said nothing.

I'd always assumed that there was some gimmick behind Nishinaka's card tricks and that one day he'd be exposed. But this time I was totally on his side – I felt like his promoter, his trainer in the ring, before a slightly hostile audience. I wanted my man to win. Come on, I prompted him silently, it must be the joker. For God's sake, man, speak up!

I found Nishinaka's concentration almost too painful to behold. His forehead was wet; I wanted to offer him my handkerchief. 'I don't understand it,' he mumbled. 'It's not a number card, no figure ... it's not the joker ...'

Not the joker? I thought. What the hell is left?

'...I've never seen such a card ... it's black ... there's writing on it ... but I can't read it.' Suddenly he rose towering over all of us who were sitting around the low coffee table. He sounded angry, not defeated. 'Show me the card,' he commanded brusquely.

I looked at the Nobel prize winner. His face was flushed as he reached for the stack of cards and slowly searched through them. Finally he found the card. He stared at it momentarily, then threw it on the table – face up – and abruptly left the room.

All of the men, except Nishinaka, bent forward to look at the card. When I saw it, I was amazed. 'Jiko, you were right. It's not really a playing card; it's just a promotion for this brand of cards. They stick it into all the new decks before they're wrapped.'

Nishinaka just glanced at me. It was neither triumph nor pleasure that I saw in his face. 'No wonder I couldn't read him,' he blurted out, 'the man's jealousy always got in the way.'

MASKENFREIHEIT

I'm a very fast reader, a skimmer really. I never wade through the documents before the board meeting begins; I go over them quickly while Rodney Hohmann, the company's chief financial officer, is still clearing his throat and shuffling his papers. I'm through before he has covered a tenth of his presentation; then I'm ready with my 'outsider's' questions, which the inside directors, who are also part of management, must take seriously, like it or not. I would never want my fellow directors to know how little preparation I do, but this morning I realized that I would have to pay the penalty of strict attention because I had left the board book at home.

Unfortunately, Rod is a classic droner. After a brief struggle, I let my thoughts go to the preceding night's dinner with Sylvia, who was home from Berkeley. Sylvia liked German, she had said, because nouns could easily be combined to produce new ones, which, though not found in any dictionary, were 'perfectly kosher'. Such *ad hoc* combinations were a concise way of describing complicated concepts for which one would need at least a sentence in English. 'Take *Maskenfreiheit*,' she announced, with a touch of aggressive amusement. 'Heine wanted to describe the freedom acquired by wearing a mask, so he simply strung together the German words for "masks" and "freedom". Here's another one:

Lebensweisheitspielerei: life's-wisdom-playfulness.'

'What about it?'

'It,' she said, 'was used by Wallace Stevens!'

'Ah,' I offered, remembering a fragment from English 3B, 'The Emperor of Ice Cream.'

'Dad, *everybody* knows "The Emperor of Ice Cream"! But not *Lebensweisheitspielerei* – you should look it up.'

I am rather proud of my daughter; but after dessert, I tried to regain my dignity. I asked as innocently as I could, 'doesn't *Maskenweisheitspielerei* lead to *Lebensfreiheit*?'

'What did you say?' Sylvia sounded downright suspicious.

Afraid I was mispronouncing, I decided to deliver the punch line myself. 'The wise playfulness associated with wearing a mask leads to freedom in life, doesn't it?'

'Papa!' she exclaimed – she calls me Papa very rarely – and threw her arms around me. '*Ausgezeichnet*! Papa, you're just like me. When I'm curious about something, I want to follow it all the way. Did you know I got interested in the history of masquerades? I started with Byron's letters from Venice. Papa, you've got to read some of that stuff.' And then she informed me that the Venetians not only wore masks to hide their identities; it was clearly understood by everyone that in such disguise, boundaries of accepted behaviour could be crossed with impunity. 'Do you know, Papa,' Sylvia said, pushing her chair closer to mine, 'if somebody in Venice didn't have his mask with him, he could wear a small lapel insignia to indicate that he wanted to be *considered* as wearing a mask. When his friends saw that sign, they actually pretended not to recognize him!'

As Rod Hohmann plodded along, this struck me.

Behind my director's mask, my non-director *persona* was off limits. For the first time in two years on the board, I studied the other men. Six white shirts (counting my own), two blue ones, and one tan sport shirt (Robert Claxton's). Five with deep red ties, the company logo discreetly woven into the fabric – a Christmas gift to all the directors; three striped Countess Mara ties, and one ascot. I realized that I'd never seen Bob Claxton with a tie. Turtlenecks in the winter, open shirts with ascots – or on occasion no neckwear – the rest of the year. Six pairs of glasses, five horn-rimmed or set in silver or gold, one (Claxton's) rimless and connected to his ears with very thin flexible straps – cat gut or strong silk thread, I guess – which were practically invisible, almost like a pince-nez.

The virtual absence of rings surprised me. Except for the chairman, who wore a small signet ring on his pinkie, and me with my wedding ring, all the directors were ringless. I'd assumed that most were married, but why was I so sure? Our conversations had never turned to families. All I really knew of the rest was what I'd read in the annual proxy statements: age, education, stock ownership, principal occupation, other board memberships. They were strangers, middle-aged or older, although they addressed me – and I them – by first names, as if we were buddies from way back.

Claxton was clearly the odd man out. And his behaviour was even odder. The rest of the men were focusing, or pretending to, on Hohmann's presentation. A couple were doodling and one was having trouble swallowing yawns, but this was acceptable director's behaviour. Claxton was continually writing in a stenographer's notebook, every once in a while looking up at Hohmann, as if catching some particular phrase. He sat across from me, on the other curve of the oval, left elbow on the table and cheek in hand, so as to shield completely the notebook from his neighbour on the left. Everybody else was looking towards the speaker at the head of the table; I was the only one watching Claxton. Each time he looked up, I closed my eyes. At board meetings you're always given the benefit of the doubt: closed eyelids are meant to imply deep concentration.

I realized that I had not the foggiest idea what Hohmann had been talking about. I hadn't paid attention, nor had I skimmed ahead through the board book. I decided to borrow Claxton's, so I slipped him a note. He hardly looked up from his scribbling as he pushed the book across the table. As I turned the pages, looking for the financial report, I came on two loose sheets. The first sentence sprang right off the page:

'Well, Nicholas, what is your definition of friendship?'

I stopped and glanced at Bob. His head was bent over the page on which he was writing, rapidly. I tilted the board book up at an angle so that neither Claxton nor Dan Lazare on my right could see what I was reading.

What is my definition, Nicholas Kahnweiler's definition, of a friend? Does the word have gender? Is there a difference between an ovarian and a testicular friend? Of course there is. What, then, is my definition of a male friend? I have just thought of one, but I won't tell him that yet, it might put him off. It's simple: a friend is a person in whose presence you can weep, who is not embarrassed by your tears. Even shedding a few tears is significant, but weeping, real weeping, counts. Have I ever cried in a man's presence? I really don't remember. Oh, I've had tears welling up in my eyes – especially in the theatre – but when did I cry?

I never cried in front of Manya – only to myself, after she left. What I was really crying about was the misery of our marriage, what it could've been but never became. But that doesn't count, that is precisely the point I'm trying to make about friends. Crying to yourself is a physiological response, or a manifestation of self-pity. An adult crying in front of another adult is – no, not 'is' but 'can be' – a form of unveiling in which men rarely engage. If, just if, someone should touch you while you cry, a hand on your shoulder is enough.

The man broke into Kahnweiler's introspection. 'Nick, if you can't think of a definition, what about a person whom you can trust without reservation?'

I'd better stop talking to myself. 'Tell me,' I said, 'do you confide in many friends?'

It was a strange combination of embarrassment and curiosity that kept me from looking at Claxton. Hohmann had finished and the group had turned to something much more exciting: a possible corporate acquisition. Even Claxton had stopped writing. I closed the board book and slid it across to him with a gesture and smile. He nodded.

The discussion became lively, but I couldn't focus on the topic. There was Claxton, asking questions as if he'd never thought about anything else. How could he switch gears so quickly? What was the connection between the two pages I'd just read and what he'd been writing until a few minutes ago?

The chairman announced the usual coffee-toilet-smoking break. I realized that here was an opportunity for some *Maskenfreiheit* research.

'Bob,' I asked, 'are you staying overnight in the city?'

'Yes,' he replied. 'Why do you ask?' It was the

closest thing to a personal conversation that we'd had since he joined the board.

'Well, I thought if you didn't have a commitment tonight, I'd ask you to join Hilary and me for dinner at home.'

'At home?' There was an awkward silence. Finally he said, 'Why, that's very nice of you.' I wondered whether curiosity or loneliness had made him accept. Or was he being polite?

Claxton rang the bell at exactly seven o'clock, as if he'd been standing behind the door checking his watch. By the time I reached the front door, Hilary and Bob were already exchanging introductions. She held a wrapped bottle of wine in her hand.

'Shall we open this for dinner?' she asked.

'As you wish.' He sounded both formal and impatient as if he wanted to dispense with all social preambles. While Hilary was still in the kitchen, Claxton wandered around the living-room like a commissar in charge of cultural evaluations. The pictures on the walls elicited no comment, but he pulled a book from the shelves. 'Did you like *Herzog*?'

'*Herzog*?' He handed over the book.

'I'm afraid I haven't read it.'

'Have you read any Bellow?' he continued.

'No.'

'But you have several of his books.' He pointed to a shelf. 'Why do you bother having them here?'

'Hilary and Sylvia, my daughter, are the fiction readers in the family,' I replied.

'What do *you* read?' Claxton stressed the second word in what seemed a mocking way. I was about to object when Hilary announced dinner.

As we started on the salad, Hilary spoke up. 'Mr

Claxton, my husband hasn't told me anything about you except that you're on the same board.'

'You see, Bob,' I interrupted, 'we've hardly touched base since I came home.'

Claxton responded with a faint smile.

'How long have the two of you known each other?' my wife continued.

'Over a year, haven't we, Bob? As I recall, you joined the board last December.'

'I have a feeling your wife wants a more precise answer, Oliver.' There was something artful about his smile as he addressed Hilary. 'Oliver and I have known each other for a total of about sixteen hours. Isn't that right, Oliver? Our board meetings don't really last longer than four hours.'

I knew that this was the sort of answer Hilary appreciated: precise, but touched with a flavour of flippancy.

'Tell me, Oliver,' Hilary began. She usually calls me 'Ollie'. 'Oliver' put me on edge. 'How much do you really learn about each other at such board meetings? My husband belongs to lots of boards,' she'd turned again to Claxton, 'but he usually doesn't talk about what transpires.'

'Good for you!' The exclamation was addressed to me; Claxton's warmth surprised me.

'Do you get to know each other at all in sixteen hours spread over a year?' Hilary persisted.

'No, we're Venetians. We wear masks at our board.' I thought I was being clever, but I realized that Sylvia's attentions to Papa last night had caused me to forget that Mama had also been present at her lecture.

'Are these masks a director's fringe benefit?' asked Hilary.

Claxton seemed to be getting more animated. 'That's a very good point. I'm sure most of us wear masks at such meetings. I certainly do.'

'Haven't you wondered what's behind some of these masks?' The challenge was thrown at both of us.

Again Claxton answered first. 'On occasion, yes.'

'What about today's meeting?'

'No, not today.'

I don't know what made me say, 'Bob was busy writing.'

He gave me a brief, searching look. 'So you noticed?'

'I couldn't help noticing,' I said. 'You sat across from me and you were writing most of the time.'

'Did you wonder what I was writing?'

'Sure I did.' I tried to be offhand. 'You were writing all the time in that peculiar notebook.'

'Peculiar?'

'Well,' I replied, 'it was a stenographer's notebook and there were yellow pads in front of all of us. I figured you couldn't possibly be making continuous notes on Hohmann's presentation. It was just too dull.'

Claxton tugged on the strings of his glasses. 'Oliver, does the name Kahnweiler mean anything to you?'

I blush rarely, but now I felt myself colouring. 'Hmm, let me think,' I offered, rising from my chair. 'Hilary, I'll clear the salad plates and bring the casserole. You keep our guest amused.'

The interval was sufficient to erase my blush; the effect, I reflected, of having your mask yanked off your face in front of witnesses. It gave me time to come up with a plausible response to the Kahnweiler question.

'You asked about Kahnweiler, Bob,' I said in a voice which insinuated that this was a simple, everyday type of question. 'Wasn't he Picasso's first dealer? I always forget his first name. Was it Daniel-Henry or Henry-Daniel?'

'Daniel-Henry,' interposed Hilary. But then she went on, 'Ollie is a collector of esoterica. Doesn't he show it at your board meetings?'

'Well,' Bob's smile seemed rather forced, 'he does ask a lot of detailed questions, but they always seem to deal with business. Nothing esoteric as far as I can recall. But tell me about Oliver the collector.'

'Ollie doesn't collect *things*,' said Hilary, referring to me as if I were absent, 'but *information*. There are times when I think he has a giant pin-cushion into which he sticks all those obscure items. I have a feeling that these pinheads contain microchips that can store a lot of information. At the right time, Oliver just picks up a pin and inserts it into his personal computer.' She tapped me on the head, a little condescendingly, I felt.

'Now it's your turn, Mr Claxton,' continued Hilary. 'What were you writing this morning?'

'Tell me,' he asked Hilary, as if he hadn't heard her question, 'do you have many friends?'

'Yes, I suppose so,' she replied cautiously. 'But what makes you ask?'

'Intimate ones?'

'Yes. Some are intimate friends.' Hilary was getting annoyed.

'Both women and men?'

I looked at Hilary, who had started to colour. 'Mostly women.'

'What about Oliver?'

'Oliver? He's my husband!'

'I know that,' said Claxton. 'But husbands or wives are not necessarily intimate friends.'

'Tell me, Mr Claxton, are you married?' Good old Hilary was going on the offensive.

'No,' he replied quietly. 'I'm divorced.'

'I see,' said Hilary as if she were addressing a witness in front of a jury and had just made her point. 'Any children?'

'Two.'

'How old?'

'Are they boys or girls?' I interjected. I had no idea what Hilary was driving at, but at least I could pretend that I did.

'Both are girls. Eighteen and twenty-one.'

'Are they your friends?' Hilary was calming down.

'Yes, I would say so.'

'Intimate ones?'

'I guess this depends on one's definition of intimacy,' he countered.

'So what is your definition of intimacy, Mr Claxton?'

'That's a good question, isn't it, Oliver?' Bob hadn't changed the tone of his voice.

'Well, it's a pretty complicated one,' I said. But Hilary came to the rescue.

'Come on, you two. Don't complicate a simple issue: an intimate friend is a person in whom you can confide; whom you can always ask for help without feeling uncomfortable.'

Again Claxton pulled on the strings of his glasses. I'd never seen him do this at board meetings. 'I had another definition of intimate friendship – primarily between males – but I have no quarrel with yours. One last question. May I?'

'Go ahead.'

'Using your definition, is Oliver an intimate friend? Do you confide in him?'

'Of course.' Hilary's answer came instantaneously.

'Really? You always confide in him?'

Slowly Hilary turned toward me, her full gaze focusing on my eyes. 'No, not always,' she said without looking away.

I was flabbergasted by the direction this dinner conversation had taken. Why, I wondered, had I been foolhardy enough to invite a virtual stranger to what was rapidly turning into a *masque à trois*? But I was in no mood to be questioned myself. I headed for the kitchen; slowly I took the coffee beans out of the freezer compartment and filled the electric coffee grinder. I put the burner on medium so that the water would take a few more minutes to come to the boil, and moved to the kitchen doorway. For the moment I preferred the role of listener.

'A novel? You, a corporate director? Actually, what do you do when you're not a director?'

'I'm working on a novel, my first.'

'What made you do it?'

'I guess I wanted to analyse myself publicly, behind the mask of a *roman-à-clef*, but now I'm enamoured by metaphors and style. For a change, I want to write something where style counts – not the usual technical business verbiage. I've been looking at some books by real craftsmen. I guess I'm trying to prime my pump.'

'Is there much water in your well?' Hilary was passably good at repartee.

'That remains to be seen; the pump hasn't run long enough. But here's the kind of thing I notice. I just reread Saul Bellow's *Herzog*. I know you've read it.'

'How do you know that?'

'Oliver told me so before dinner.'

'Ollie? Why in heaven should he have told you that?'

'Just ask your intimate friend. I read *Herzog* slower

and slower, until it took me several minutes to complete one page. I stopped at each sentence; I asked myself, how did the man think of this phrase? At one point Bellow is talking about an old bathtub – a trivial enough object that hasn't much to do with the story – and describes its enamel edge as "wreathed with hairlike twistings, like cooked rhubarb". I decided I'd see how I would have said this, but I just got stuck in the vegetable patch: "cooked celery" is all I came up with.'

'Celery hair isn't as thin as rhubarb hair,' interrupted Hilary.

Claxton broke into laughter. 'You see, you're getting caught in the same net. Of course you're right. Then I thought of cooked salsify.'

'Salsify? What's that?'

'That's exactly the trouble with salsify. It's too clever. Rhubarb is common; everyone knows what it is, but few would've used it as a metaphor to describe hairlike twistings.'

As I put the coffee pot, cups, saucers, and an open bottle of port with three glasses on the tray, I could still hear Claxton's animated voice in the living-room. Through the open kitchen door I saw the two of them sitting next to each other on the sofa. Something in me made me stop at the doorway again.

'Take one of my favourite poets, Wallace Stevens. Occasionally I make up combinations of individual words that Stevens used in his curious way. What do you think of *aspic aplomb*?' Claxton waited. I could see Hilary's right hand playing with her hair.

'You mean "there was aspic aplomb in her eyes"?' she asked.

'Is that what your eyes are saying, Hilary? I wouldn't have guessed.'

Hilary wasn't prepared to commit herself. 'What did Stevens write, Bob?'

'First tell me your association – quickly – with the word "aspic".'

'Tongue.'

'Tongue?'

'Tongue quivering in aspic. Haven't you eaten cold tongue in aspic?'

'What word would you guess Stevens combined with aspic?'

'Tell me.' Hilary was going for the bait.

'Nipples.'

'Nipples? Aspic nipples? You mean nipples that quiver?'

Claxton laughed again. 'Hilary, I take a bow. That's how I originally interpreted it. But Stevens would've been shocked. I think it's our post-Freudian sexual fantasizing: aspic quivers, breasts quiver, when you eat aspic you almost suck it in, sucking nipples …'

'Stop it, Bob.' Hilary giggled. 'What did he mean?'

'Bitter nipples. Exactly the opposite. The line goes something like, "How is it that your aspic nipples for once vent honey?"'

'I like the ambiguity of "aspic".' Why doesn't Hilary leave the topic? I thought. 'How about "the quivering aspic of her pupils"?' she continued. 'Come on, Bob, just look at my aspic eyes.'

'I am, Hilary,' he said.

The tray in my hands tilted slightly, rattling the cups. Claxton's voice stopped in mid-sentence.

Hilary turned around casually. 'What took you so long, Ollie?' Addressing Claxton, she added, 'You should see how quickly he makes coffee in the morning.'

My God, I thought, she does have aplomb. As I put

the tray on the coffee table, I asked, 'What were you two talking about while I was slaving away in the kitchen?'

'Bob was just telling me about your meeting this morning.' I had never realized how smooth Hilary could be.

I tried to be nonchalant, unsuccessfully. 'What specifically?'

'Oh, just chit-chat.' Of course, nobody confides totally *all* of the time, I thought. Still ...

'Let me bring some cookies,' she said brightly, and escaped into the kitchen.

'Cream and sugar?' I asked Claxton.

'No thanks, just black.' And then he took me by surprise. 'Oliver, your response earlier on about Kahnweiler was clever, but you do know why I asked you that question, don't you?'

'Yes,' I replied. 'Do you want some port?'

'Then why did you answer it that way?'

'What did you want me to say in front of Hilary?'

'What's wrong with the truth?'

'How about some port?'

'Did you read all of it?' he persisted.

I nodded.

'Why?'

'Come on, Bob. What would you've done if you'd opened the board book and found those pages?'

'I would've closed it immediately and returned it to you.'

I was about to tell him that I didn't believe it when Hilary reappeared. 'Chocolate mints, anybody?' she asked, as she brought in a plate, the dark brown squares arranged in a spiral shape. Hilary pays attention to the appearance of such things. I took two, but Claxton raised a hand, palm up, like a traffic policeman.

'You two look as if you'd been talking business.'

'We were,' I said.

'Too bad.' It's amazing how at times two words can be full of ambiguous meaning.

Claxton looked at her. 'It was connected with masks – the kind that give you freedom. The question is, what right does a man have to look behind a mask without the bearer's permission?'

'What was your answer, Ollie?' she asked.

'We hadn't gotten to that yet,' interjected Claxton. 'If Oliver doesn't mind my doing it in front of you, for a change I'd like to take a look behind his mask.'

'For a change?'

'Tell me, Oliver, what's your definition of friendship?'

It wasn't the question I had expected. 'I hadn't thought of it,' I said, 'but I guess I agree with yours.'

This seemed to mollify Claxton, who started to pour himself some port. But it didn't satisfy Hilary. How could it? 'For heaven's sake,' she exclaimed, 'what are the two of you talking about?'

For a moment Claxton and I looked at each other, and allowed ourselves to laugh.

Hilary didn't appreciate her abrupt and involuntary transformation into an outsider. 'You know, your boards are really like fraternities. I never hear you mention any women, Oliver.'

The bubble of male conviviality was punctured. 'I'm sorry, Hilary, of course we should tell you.'

But then Claxton asked, 'Hilary, do you keep a journal?'

'Yes,' she said. 'I've kept one for years. Why do you ask?'

There was Hilary, to whom I've been married for twenty-six years, announcing to a virtual stranger something that I, her husband, never even got a clear answer about whenever I asked what she was writing.

'I thought so. In that case,' continued Claxton, 'I'd like to ask both of you a question.'

He pulled out his notebook, tore out two pages, handed one to each of us, and his pen to Hilary. 'Oliver, do you happen to have a pen?' I reached into my jacket. 'Would the two of you write down your answer – just a simple yes or no – to the following question. Suppose you walked into a room, here in your house, and inadvertently found an open notebook lying on the table. Suppose further, you took a look at one of the pages and realized instantly that it was the private diary of your spouse. Incidentally, Oliver, for argument's sake, I'm assuming that you're also the keeper of a journal. Are you in fact?'

'No, never.'

He ignored me. 'Knowing now that you're looking at your spouse's private diary, would you continue reading it? Remember, you're not being observed; you're alone in the room.'

Before I could protest, Hilary had scribbled her answer, folded the paper, and handed it over to Claxton. Trapped, I did likewise.

Claxton shuffled the two sheets in a rather ostentatious manner and then unfolded them. 'I thought so,' he said. 'Come Hilary, explain your answer to the fraternity jocks.'

'What is there to explain? Of course I wouldn't have continued reading the diary. What do you take me for? It would've been an unforgivable intrusion into Oliver's privacy. I don't think I could live with somebody who'd do that.'

'Don't get angry, Hilary. I feel the same way as you do. I just wanted to hear it from you out loud.'

That's all he said, with the two pieces of paper still in his hand.

'Aren't you going to ask Ollie?' But Claxton had now taken the two pages, lined them up, one on top of the other, and folded them in half. He ran them a couple of times between thumb and index finger to make a sharp crease and then extracted from his jacket pocket a fat Swiss army knife. He used the scissors to cut out a triangular wedge half way along the fold and a second straight one, an eighth of an inch long, just below it. Carefully, he shaped the top of the folded sheet into a half moon. For a moment, he inspected his handiwork and then, using the end of the scissors, he poked a hole through the upper portion of the folded papers. Hilary seemed mesmerized by the performance.

Finally, he separated the two sheets and partly unfolded them. 'There you are,' he announced as he set them in front of our coffee cups. 'A mask for each of you!'

It was true. It was almost spooky how these two pieces of paper, with our one-word answers on the back, had been transformed into two identical masks; the final stab with the scissors had produced the eyes.

I'd been thinking of how I'd explain my answer. I wanted to be candid and point out that my 'yes' simply meant that satisfying one's curiosity was neither devious nor premeditated. Still, I was grateful that the matter seemed dropped.

'Hilary,' Claxton said, 'earlier on you seemed annoyed when we both laughed at you. I think we laughed for the same reason: embarrassment.'

'Come on, Bob ...' I began, but Hilary cut me off.

'Why were you people embarrassed?'

'At dinner time I told you that I had a different definition of friendship from yours, primarily because I had been thinking of friendship between men. That's the theme of the novel I've been working on.'

Now it became my turn to interrupt. 'How come you're writing fiction at a board meeting?' There I was at the meeting, behaving and dressing like a proper director; and there was Claxton in his own private world, just because he was wearing a director's mask. Did he actually have the gall to think that he was earning his director's fee while diverting himself with his damn novel?

'But why not, Ollie?' cried out Hilary. 'Didn't you tell us earlier how dull you'd found the man's presentation? What was his name?'

'Hohmann,' Claxton said, enjoying himself.

'Listen, you two directors,' remarked Hilary, 'let's all forget about the board meeting. What I want to know is your definition of friendship. From both of you!'

Claxton looked at his watch. 'It's getting late,' he announced, 'and I still want to do a bit of writing in my journal. Oliver can tell you all about friendship and you can tell him about director's masks. Or maybe the other way around.'

After seeing Claxton off, I offered to take care of the dishes, but Hilary insisted that we return to the sofa. I shrugged and followed her into the living-room. As I sat down, I noticed that she was staring at the miniature paper masks standing in front of our coffee cups. I was about to ask whether she wanted more coffee, but it was too late.

'Ollie, why on earth did he make these little masks?' she asked slowly as she turned over the one in front of her cup, the mask on which I had written my answer to Claxton's question. 'They give me the creeps.'

FIRST-CLASS NUN

In his frequent interviews Michael Brewis made a fetish out of eye contact. He first judged the calibre of his clients by the way they held out against his penetrating stare; only then came a scrutiny of their conversational savoir-faire. But he always avoided eye contact on airplanes. It was his way of announcing that he was not available for casual chit-chat. On this flight, as he walked down the aisle to find his assigned seat, he was gratified to note that he had no neighbour; the distant gaze, the fixed stare at the page, the pretence at dozing – none of these, it seemed, would be necessary. He had just placed his open briefcase on the empty seat beside him, however, when he heard a woman's low voice. 'Excuse me. I believe this is my seat.'

Brewis was so annoyed he barely looked up as he gathered his papers and closed the briefcase. Without a further word, the woman slipped into her seat; she opened a book before he'd even started on his papers. Soon after take-off, the stewardess came around offering a dinner menu, which he stuffed, unread, into the seat pocket. He always ordered a special meal ahead of time, usually a vegetarian dish or a fresh-fruit plate. On this occasion he had decided on fruit for the trip to New York and a vegetarian platter for the return to San Francisco. Even though he was concentrating on his paperwork, he waited for the second interruption, the stewardess's question, 'Have you chosen your dinner entrée?' But when the question came, it was addressed to his neighbour, not to him.

'Sister Olivia Fitzsimmons?'
'Yes?'
'Did you order the special vegetarian dinner?'
'Yes, I did, thank you.'
'Would you like anything to drink before dinner?'
'Do you have any white wine?'
'Yes, a California Riesling and white Zinfandel.'
'No Chardonnay?'
'I'm afraid not.'
'In that case, just some soda water with lime.'

Brewis finally looked sideways at his companion. Sister? British nurses are called sister, he thought, but the accent was east-coast USA with a slight southern nuance. A nun? I've never met a nun, or even seen one in first class. How come she's so choosy about the wine? Is that what they drink in their cells?

His silent questions were interrupted by the stewardess: 'What can I bring you, sir?'

'I've also ordered a vegetarian dinner.'

'Oh, there must be a mistake, we were given only one for this trip.'

'But I ordered it weeks ago,' protested Brewis. 'I always order it when I make my reservations.'

'I'm terribly sorry, sir. Somebody must've goofed.'

'Perhaps I'm responsible for this mistake,' interjected his neighbour. 'I only ordered mine yesterday. Why don't you take it? I'll order something else.'

'No, I wouldn't think of it,' replied Brewis. 'It's very kind of you.' He turned to the stewardess. 'I'll have the fish.'

'What will you have to drink?' asked the stewardess.

'Nothing right now.' He hardly ever drank on plane trips, but he was aware that his refusal in this case sounded petulant.

As the stewardess left, Brewis's neighbour remarked in a low voice: 'You're irritated, aren't you? It's not really worth it – maybe the fish will surprise you.'

Brewis had turned to the woman; he was not accustomed to being evaluated. For the first time he studied her carefully. He couldn't tell much about her body – she was dressed in a brown wrap-around skirt, her legs out of sight, a light-brown, high-buttoned long-sleeved blouse covering most of her torso. She wore no jewellery except for a necklace with a silver cross, and absolutely no make-up. He focused on her face: light brown hair, pulled tight around her head into a bun; flawless complexion; full lips; and wide-open, intensely green eyes.

'You look as if you're about to ask me a question.' A hint of a smile had crept into her eyes. 'Why don't you go ahead?'

Again Brewis was taken aback. He, the professional questioner, was not used to being prompted. 'You're right. When the stewardess addressed you as "Sister", I first thought of an English nurse, but as soon as you spoke …'

'You mean my accent?'

'Yes, and something in your tone. I concluded that you must be a nun, but, well, you don't look like one.'

'You mean I don't wear a nun's habit and I'm not holding a prayer book?'

'I didn't look at your book.'

'Well, look at it.'

Brewis took one glance at the proffered book cover. *The Church and The Second Sex*? I've heard about it. Are you interested in feminist ideology?'

'Very much. And how do you know that Mary Daly is a feminist?'

Brewis was pleased by the unexpected aggressiveness. 'I'm interested in women,' he replied, 'in the role they're playing in contemporary society, and especially the roles they should play.' He realized how stilted this sounded. He added, 'Are you surprised?'

'Actually, yes.'

'But then I have to admit that I'm surprised to find a nun reading such books.'

'You don't know much about nuns, do you? Some of us live in the present.' The green eyes sparkled as she continued, 'Now that you've met your first one, you're burning to ask the next question, aren't you?'

'Yes.' He enjoyed being egged on. 'When did you become a nun? What made you do it?'

'In my twenties, after I finished graduate school, in philosophy.'

The nun looked too playful, somehow too worldly, to be a philosopher, Brewis thought. 'What made you decide to go from graduate school to a ...?'

'You're hesitating,' observed the nun. 'Is it because you're thinking of a nunnery but don't want to say it? You could always call it a convent.'

How does this woman manage to maintain the offensive? he thought. Some philosopher! 'You seem to anticipate everything I'm about to say.'

'Not really. It's just that we hear this all the time, especially from men.'

There was a bantering undertone to her remark; he decided to be formal. 'Sister, don't embarrass me. It's just that "convent" has a medieval ring to it that doesn't fit you. You're dressed conservatively – but you're not in a nun's habit; you could be an everyday woman, and a very handsome one at that.'

She laughed openly. 'You really do have all the stereotypical responses. You mean a nun can't or shouldn't be attractive? Besides, you've really only seen my face.'

Brewis didn't even begin to rationalize his faux pas nor her utterly secular response; he quickly shifted gears. 'But you travel first-class; you're choosy about what wine you drink – somehow I don't associate any of this with a convent, most certainly not with a nunnery.'

'You're right,' replied the nun after a moment's hesitation, 'about the first-class seat. Just to set the record straight: we always travel economy-class. This time United had oversold, and when I told them that I simply had to get to San Francisco tonight for an engagement that I could not break' – to his surprise, the nun blushed as she pronounced the word "engagement" – 'they put me in this empty seat.'

Brewis finally saw his opening. 'Tell me,' he asked innocently, 'how come the stewardess called you sister? How did she know you were a nun?'

'How did she know?' echoed the nun and looked out the window. After an awkward pause she rushed on. 'When the agent at the gate told me that I should've checked in earlier, I explained that I had trouble getting a cab at the convent. The moment I mentioned the word "convent", he changed his tune. He handed me over to the stewardess and told her to "be sure to take extra care of Sister Olivia".' She shrugged her shoulders. 'You see, I was not pulling rank.'

Brewis wasn't ready to let go. 'What about the rest – your dress, the wine, the book you read?'

'That only shows how little you know about nuns.'

'I know nothing about them. Actually, I know very little about religious life; you're talking to an agnostic from way back.'

'Let me guess,' retorted the nun. 'You must be a scientist. Am I right?'

'No, but what makes you say this?'

'The almost aggressive tone in which you said "agnostic from way back". If you don't mind my asking, what's your occupation?'

'I'm a headhunter,' he said matter-of-factly.

'You're what?'

It was not the first time he'd heard such a response when he used that term to describe his occupation. 'I run an executive search agency. I interview people for top management jobs.'

'Is this how you interview people – the way you're questioning me?'

For a moment, Brewis gazed at the nun as if to determine whether there was more to her remark, and then his eyes wandered, past the woman, through the plane window to the wing flaps shuddering in the jet stream.

'No,' he said slowly, 'I'm not interviewing you. But I'd like to know something about a nun's life – I mean your present life. What brought you there?'

It was her turn to study him. 'All right,' she said finally, 'it won't hurt an agnostic headhunter to learn something about nuns. You probably think only of the dictionary definition of a nun – a woman belonging to a religious order, living in a convent under vows of obedience, poverty and chastity. Have you heard of the Order of the Carmelites?'

'Yes. But what's special about them?'

'I'll try to make it brief. The origin of our order is somewhat uncertain, but can probably be traced back to a twelfth-century retreat on Mount Carmel. Incidentally, the Carmelite houses are called monasteries, not convents. Because of our hermit origin and emphasis on solitude, no more than twenty-one nuns live in any one monastery, each occupying her own cell. Nobody else enters such a cell, only the prioress, and she must be invited. This is very different from other orders, say the Benedictine, in which several hundred nuns may live in one convent and sleep in dormitories.' Suddenly, she stopped. 'I must sound like a tourist guide. Tell me, are you really interested in such details?'

'Yes, I'm fascinated. But I'm wondering when you're going to get around to explaining what you're doing in that dress.'

The nun nodded eagerly, as if her tourist guide licence depended on her reply. 'Most of the time we wear brown, but as you can see by looking at me we don't necessarily wear a nun's habit. Of course, we're not fashion plates. We buy sensible skirts, blouses, sandals – what I'm wearing now was ordered largely out of an L.L. Bean catalogue.'

Brewis's amused expression produced another blush in her face. For some unexplained reason he felt pleased. 'Please, go on.'

'Our house in Brooklyn is one of the more modern ones. There are others, not far from ours, which do not differ much from the Carmelite monasteries of several centuries ago.'

'What do the nuns do in your monastery?'

'It depends on the house,' replied Sister Olivia. 'Some lead a very cloistered life, not unlike what the general public thinks nuns do. Others are very different. In our Brooklyn house there are nineteen nuns, and you'd be surprised how diverse their backgrounds and interests are. I am supposed to be a spiritual counsellor ...'

'You, a counsellor?' The term unsettled Brewis. Only a few days ago, his wife Claire had announced that he should see a therapist. 'Damned shrinks,' he'd sputtered. 'What are they going to tell me that I don't already know?'

'I am a counsellor – largely for outsiders who wish guidance or advice.' She hurried on, as if she were wishing to change the subject. 'Among my fellow nuns are a photographer and a musician.'

In spite of his alerted caution, Brewis couldn't refrain. 'I suppose Poulenc is her favourite?'

'Why?' The nun seemed nonplussed.

'You know, the *Dialogue of the Carmelites*.' Michael Brewis frequently indulged in what his wife used to call 'cultural braggadocio'. Claire hadn't meant it as a compliment, but he couldn't drop the habit.

The woman looked at him anxiously, as if caught unprepared. 'I'm afraid I don't understand.'

Brewis might have persisted in showing off, but this time he resisted the temptation. 'Oh, never mind. What other occupations do you have?'

She seemed relieved. 'We have a couple of writers and run a small press. You were surprised about my reading. Of course, we live with the Bible and with religious books, but our concept of spiritual and religious literature is a broad one.'

'Sister, your mention of books has triggered a question in my mind.' He turned to face her more directly, as he always did when he searched for information. 'Those vows you mentioned – I'm curious about them. Let's start with obedience: how does that jibe with that feminist book you're reading?'

'Let me start with poverty, which refers to worldly possessions,' countered the nun. 'Really we lead a rich life; rich in content and rich in privacy. If you're interested in intellectual or spiritual endeavours, modern life offers you little time or place for contemplation. That, and companionship with kindred spirits, with other women, are important, especially in this male-dominated world. Incidentally, this is one reason why some nuns are interested in feminist ideology. Why not? After all, we're all women, and the role of women in the Church is now a topic of hot debate, at least in some religious circles. Now do you see why I'm reading Mary Daly's book?'

He persisted. 'I understand, Sister, but then let me ask how you handle poverty of possessions. For instance, you were rather emphatic with the stewardess about wanting Chardonnay. Are you a wine connoisseur? And if you are, how did you, a nun, become one? How does all this fit in with poverty?'

'You sound a bit like a district attorney ...'

'I didn't mean to,' protested Brewis.

'I'm just joking,' said the nun. 'Of course you're justified in asking about the wine. I joined the Carmelites when I was twenty-six years old and my parents frequently had wine at dinner. In addition, my father-in-law was a wine importer ...'

Brewis was so surprised that he couldn't restrain himself. 'Your father-in-law?'

'Yes, I was married before I joined the order.' The brevity of her reply made clear that this was not a topic to be pursued.

'Occasionally, we have wine at dinner at the monastery, but cheap jug-wine. In a way I'm glad the stewardess had no Chardonnay – there is no reason to remind oneself of an earlier life that one has left voluntarily ...'

Her voice trailed off as she sipped on the glass of soda-water. Suddenly, looking straight ahead, she began again, in such a low voice that Brewis strained to hear.

'In a way, I'm being tested all the time by temptations from my past. Not in the big ways you might imagine, but in little ones that most people don't even think about. It's particularly true at meal times. It's not just the wine, it's items like cheese or fish. For instance, we always eat processed cheese in the monastery; many a time my mouth waters for a good strong Stilton or Camembert. But when my turn comes to do the shopping, I also return with Velveeta, even though I could've saved money on some other purchases and bought a more interesting cheese. Or fish: in our house, it's almost always flounder. In fact, these days it's mostly frozen flounder, now that we have the microwave – a gift from the family of one of our nuns. You know, we get CARE packages all the time. I myself put a stop to it with my family ...'

'Really? Why?' Brewis felt disappointed.

'It was when my brother sent me some Godiva chocolates. You know, it's really trivial what I'm telling you. Temptations such as these are easily resisted ...'

'Unless you're travelling,' interrupted the smiling Brewis.

Sister Olivia looked at him as if she were searching for a hidden motive behind his comment; then she returned a fleeting smile. 'Perhaps these temptations prove that it isn't so easy to forget one's former life or even to decide what is and isn't a temptation. Especially in a modern religious house where the nuns have frequent contacts with the outside world.'

'Let me ask you about a more subtle example.' By now Brewis felt in complete command of the conversation. 'What about intellectual connoisseurship, say in books?'

They were interrupted by the stewardess, who had come to set their tables. 'Would you like some wine with your meal?' Brewis repressed a laugh and gestured to his neighbour.

The nun turned to him, amusement in her eyes, and asked, 'What would you recommend?'

That was elegantly done, he thought. Looking directly at her, he said, 'Oh, I think if I were you I'd just order water.'

Without hesitation, Sister Olivia turned to the waiting stewardess. 'I'll follow the gentleman's advice. Just water for me.'

'And you, sir?'

'Let's see. You said earlier that you had no Chardonnay, but I've forgotten what white wines you have on board.'

'Riesling and white Zinfandel,' replied the woman.

'From what vineyards?'

'They both come from Almaden.'

'Oh, in that case I'll just have water,' replied Brewis, flippantly.

As soon as the stewardess had left, Sister Olivia said, 'This little performance was for my benefit, wasn't it?'

There seemed less admonishment than amusement in the question. 'I'm sorry; I guess I was performing a bit.'

Her reply surprised him. 'There's nothing wrong

with acting, provided you stay in character.'

'Did I?'

An impish smile crossed the nun's face. 'You should be the judge.'

Michael Brewis, the experienced interviewer, decided it was time to change the subject. 'Are you free to read anything you wish? You implied – no, you said – that in your monastery the definition of religious books is a very broad one. Surely there must be some limits to that broad definition? Take some fiction that is downright anti-religious. As a nun, are you permitted to read such books? I don't mean by your prioress. Do you permit yourself exposure to such books?'

Sister Olivia had been nibbling at the salad. She turned towards her neighbour and spoke deliberately. 'There is no black-and-white answer to your question. In the more traditional Carmelite monasteries, the answer is simpler. But in our Brooklyn monastery we have much more exposure to the outside, which, of course, also includes books and other literature. In addition, our professions frequently require that we familiarize ourselves with a great deal of secular literature. My own activity as a counsellor is a case in point. To that extent, each nun must make individual judgements and sometimes that isn't easy. It's certainly more difficult than rejecting Chardonnay.'

The changes in her conversational style puzzled Brewis. Now she sounded again like a guide reciting a standard line. 'You said that each Carmelite nun has complete privacy in her cell. It seems to me that it would be very simple to, so to speak, smuggle any reading material into your cell.'

'Now just a moment,' rejoined the nun. 'You make

it sound like a girls' school, where the students are trying to circumvent the system. I've probably over-simplified the decision-making power of the individual, even in as modern a house as ours. There is a considerable amount of peer-control. If I want to purchase a book, I usually need to pay for it from our communal funds. I won't be told "Buy this book but not that one" but most of my sisters will know what book I've bought. If one of the nuns – not just the prioress – thinks that it is an inappropriate book, she'll say so. We'll then discuss it, and if a debate arises other nuns will join in. Of course, I could "smuggle" a book into my cell, as you put it, but personally I can't conceive of doing it. This doesn't alter the fundamental dilemma you've pointed out – the conflict between temptation caused by connoisseurship and our emphasis on poverty.'

Brewis nodded pensively. 'What about your other vow, obedience?'

Sister Olivia answered almost eagerly. 'That's an easy, much easier question. The outside world looks on obedience as a burden. Of course nuns are obedient to the prescriptions of their religious tenets. It's what brought them together. But primarily they're obedient to a standard of morality that's not difficult to accept if you compare it with the values of the outside world.'

'And the vow of chastity?'

'What about it? Remember, women of all ages enter the order. Some are virgins, others have led an active sexual life.' There was no hesitancy, no demure look at the floor: she kept her eyes straight on Brewis as she continued. 'They know what they're doing. Abstinence from sex is not always so enormous a sacrifice for women as many people, notably men, think.'

My God, thought Brewis, I can't believe it. Have she

and Claire been talking to each other? He felt embarrassed, but he asked the question anyway. 'Do you often talk about this subject?'

'I told you earlier that my primary function in our house is to provide counsel and that I do not just see nuns. There are no boundaries to what a counsellor discusses.'

'Do men also come to you for guidance?'

'Indeed. Why do you ask?'

Brewis just shrugged. He didn't know how to introduce the subject of Claire: the wife who was about to walk out on him. In his professional life, he was really a headhunter for men, or at least male types; the few women he'd encountered mostly fell into the same category. In his private life, Brewis hardly remembered meeting a woman where sex didn't actually or potentially enter the equation. But this was so totally different.

'You look pensive. Are you bothered by something I've said?'

'No, not at all,' he said quickly, almost apologetically. 'I was just thinking about your counselling work. I've never had any professional contact with shrinks. I'm sorry: "therapists". A verbal habit – probably some stupid reflex on the part of a supposedly strong man who thinks that he should be able to solve all of his problems by himself and that a therapist is a crutch. Or to put it another way, if you need to unburden yourself, do it with a friend.'

'There are times when a friend is the last person. Do you open up often to a friend?'

'I guess not. Perhaps it's an occupational hazard. I spend most of my time analysing others. I seem to have lost the ability or even inclination for self-analysis. Maybe it's my profession: I'm really a matchmaker, with the corporation as the bride for whom I'm interviewing suitable husbands.'

Brewis looked straight ahead. This way he could pretend that he was speaking to himself. 'As I listened to you, I was almost wondering what would happen if I, the agnostic headhunter, the impersonal matchmaker, were to talk to a spiritual counsellor.'

A sudden and remarkable change occurred in the nun's demeanor. It was as if she knew what would follow, and wanted to stop it before the question was actually raised. 'Everybody can benefit from therapy and especially from spiritual counselling,' she said. And then the curtain dropped. 'I hope you won't think me rude, but I've suddenly gotten quite tired.' With these words she reclined her seat and closed her eyes.

Brewis began to read, but he couldn't focus on the pages. He kept reflecting on what had transpired. How he'd been on the verge of making an extraordinary request to this nun: to be his shrink, to show him how to talk to his wife. According to Claire, every person has only a certain quota of understanding and he, the headhunter *par excellence*, was draining his cup of empathy daily at the office. And just when he, who usually questioned others without disclosing anything himself, was ready to relinquish his standard role, the nun entered her cell and closed the door. Brewis simply couldn't figure it out. Eventually, as the cabin darkened for the movie, he fell asleep.

The captain's voice woke him, announcing their impending landing in San Francisco. To his amazement he found that he'd slept for over two hours and that the seat next to his was empty. After a few minutes, the *no smoking* sign came on, but still no nun. Brewis looked around to see whether she had moved elsewhere in the first class cabin. At that moment, Sister Olivia reappeared and slid into her seat. He quickly turned, ready with a polite remark, but the woman seemed oblivious to his existence. Her attention was completely focused on rummaging through her bag. When Olivia Fitzsimmons finally straightened up, she caught the full force of his stare. Her smile was vaguely apologetic as she pointed to the small bottle in her left hand. 'I always have problems with my ears plugging up when we land.' Tilting back her head, she placed a few drops of decongestant into each nostril. 'I hope you had a good sleep,' she said just as the plane's wheels touched the ground.

They were among the first passengers to deplane. Brewis decided that he would ask the nun for her address. Why not bring up point blank his request about counselling? he thought. They had reached the end of the narrow gangway and were about to enter the lounge when the first light flash momentarily blinded his eyes. 'Peter, you shouldn't have,' exclaimed Sister Olivia to the man who had thrust a huge bouquet of yellow roses at her. Cradling the flowers in her right arm, she smiled smartly at the cameras with the flashbulbs popping one after another.

'Peter darling,' Brewis heard her coo, 'wait till you see the script. It's better than *Agnes of God*. You should've seen the convent ...'

WHAT'S TATIANA TROYANOS DOING IN SPARTACUS'S TENT?

Through years of sexual reality, I dreamed ever so often of a woman lover who'd sing while coupling with her man. Once a husky-voiced woman, who'd brought her guitar, started to sing in a stunning contralto. Lying on my bed, exhausted and content, gazing at the naked woman strumming her instrument, I was about to ask her whether she could ... But then I chickened out; I was afraid she'd just laugh.

Years after, I happened to go to a performance of Monteverdi's *L'incoronazione di Poppea*, set in the time of Emperor Nero before he went mad, with Tatiana Troyanos singing the lead role. About half-way through the love-scene on the couch between the young Nero and Poppea, the performance assumed such erotic overtones that I began to squirm in my seat. I don't go to operas for sexual titillation; except for an occasional *Salome* or *Lulu*, it's the music that excites me. But this was different. Suddenly I realized that Troyanos was the woman of my fantasies who'd walked into Spartacus's tent over two thousand years ago.

I was a relatively late bloomer, a virgin until nearly twenty. But as an otherwise precocious teenager, I made up for it soaking in the delicious warmth of a full bath. Not in one of those modern tubs, where even I – only five foot six – can't stretch out, so shallow that the water barely reaches one's navel, where either shoulders or feet project into the cold. No, my passions throve in a real tub – one of those huge pre-war jobs – where I'd float, water up to the chin, with soapy hands between my thighs, incandescently copulating with Veronica Thwale.

When I met that cool, severely dressed, sexual androgyne – perfumed in civet and flowers, walking down a church aisle, the *Decameron* camouflaged inside the covers of her prayer book to prove the pleasures of blasphemy – I was smitten for weeks, then months. Veronica, in her twenties, was the deftly cunning courtesan I'd been waiting for and had finally found: in Aldous Huxley's *Time Must Have a Stop*. God, she was something! Once our passion slipped me forward in that six-foot tub, so that I choked on soapy water.

But the spur to my longest and most lucid dream was *The Gladiators* – Arthur Koestler's version of the slave uprising led by Spartacus. Don't get me wrong. As time passed, as I became a man, there were months, even whole years, when Spartacus did not exist. But the vision never departed totally from my memory. When I had a lover whose climax always ended in such a long-drawn cry that we could never meet in a hotel, I wondered more than once how Spartacus handled this in his tent on the plains of Campania. And when I saw *Spartacus* at the Bolshoi in Moscow thirty-five years after I'd read Koestler's novel, I felt a pleasure reawakening.

I still remember where the scene appeared: on a left-hand page, fairly high up, three or four lines from the top. Koestler had sketched Spartacus's portrait with just a few deft strokes: the tall, slightly hunched body draped with fur-skin; his wandering eyes and cleverness; his freckles; his words that seared your ears as he spoke. And the women he had come to his tent to satisfy his sexual urges – the camp-followers, the *impedimenta*. But one evening, on that left-hand page, a woman of a different breed came to him. I, the teenage virgin, saw it clearly: the tent flap swaying as she slid in barefoot; a whiff of musk and ointment and female sweat entering with her; the chocolate skin gleaming as she passed the flickering candle; her firm breasts bearing nipples like diamonds on a ring. She kneeled beside Spartacus's reclining figure, peeled off his fur-skin and wordlessly started to caress him. For once, Spartacus took no initiative; he let the woman pleasure him. When she saw him aroused, she proceeded to sing in a low voice, mounting him – the first time Spartacus had ever been mounted – and with his phallus deep in her, she thrust faster and faster, singing more loudly, in full voice, to her climax. I know what you're thinking. But remember, I'd read Koestler's novel nearly forty years ago as an innocent youth who wanted to have his fur-skin removed.

Since *Poppea*, I've seen Troyanos in many roles, from a very male Julius Caesar in Handel's opera, or a flighty Dorabella in *Cosi Fan Tutte*, to a recent concert performance in Berlioz's *Les Nuits d'Eté*. At the end of the Berlioz, I met one of the musicians, whom I knew quite well, and told him how touched I'd been by Troyanos's singing. On the spur of the moment I spilled out the Koestler story – he's the only person who's heard it – and confessed that in Troyanos's Poppea I had finally seen the woman of my bathtub days. I even alluded to my most recent Troyanos fantasy: listening to her while we're both soaking in a hot tub. That's when he caught me by surprise. Did I want to meet Troyanos? he asked; he could arrange an introduction. 'Absolutely not,' I replied. He seemed taken aback, so I tried to explain that a life-long illusion might be destroyed. What if, screwing up my courage, I blurted out my Spartacus tale to Troyanos and asked, 'Do you sing when you make love?' She'd probably fix me with those huge dark eyes, this time full of impishness and irony, and murmur, 'Of course I do. Always.' What then? Would I've dared to mention my choice of the song I wanted to hear as she ...?

Instead, I went home and decided to re-read *The Gladiators*, which I hadn't looked at for thirty-eight years. But I couldn't even find the book; I must have lost my copy during one of my many moves. The local library didn't have it. Finally I located a worn copy at the university, a 1950 third printing by Macmillan. I took the volume home and skimmed the upper portions of the left-hand pages. That probably took half an hour, because every once in a while I stopped to read a paragraph or two. But I was so impatient to find my scene that I kept turning the pages. I found nothing. Well, I figured, maybe this edition is printed in a different format. Back I went to page one and flipped through the right-hand pages. Again nothing. It was preposterous. I'd seen Troyanos in *Poppea* and everything in me – memories of untold and untellable fantasies, embellished by the wishful inventions of late middle age – told me that she'd been in Spartacus's tent. I was prepared to concede minor imperfections in my memory: but the fact that she had mounted Spartacus and sung, *that* simply had to be there.

So I took the book to bed and read it, slowly, starting with the prologue: 'It is night still. Still no cock had crowed.' It's a great beginning and I savoured every page. That is, every page until I got to number eighty-four – a left-hand page. There in lines twelve to fourteen from the bottom, Koestler has Spartacus say these words to Crixus: *'I have never been to Alexandria. It must be a very beautiful place. Once I lay with a girl, and she sang. That is what Alexandria must be like.'*

I've never been to Alexandria, of course, and I've never lain with an Egyptian woman. But if anybody ever again offers an introduction to Tatiana Troyanos, I'll accept.

THE TOYOTA CANTOS

I still think it's absurd. There I was in the hospital, my arm in a cast, feeling sorry for myself, and still not knowing precisely how I'd smashed up Bea's car. According to the police, it was a total wreck. They just towed it to the dump. So what did I do? I didn't even wait to get home. I called my wife in Paris. 'Bea,' I said. Or maybe it was 'Bay-ah-tree-chay', which under the circumstances was probably a mistake. The first time I pronounced her name that way was at a departmental party when I was still an assistant professor. She just laughed. I guess she was humouring the budding Dante scholar. The next time around, she responded with a faint smile, but after that she just looked pained. Once, a couple of years later, she blew up: 'Goddammit, Lionel, you just married me so you could demonstrate that, like Dante, you had a Bay-ah-tree-chay.' I told her not to be silly because if that had been so I would have called her Bay-ah-tree-chay right from the beginning. Anyway, after that I tried to be careful and not overdo it.

From my hospital bed I said, 'Bay-ah-tree-chay, I'll buy you a new car. What kind do you want?' When she replied, 'I don't need a new car, I *have* one that still runs fine,' I probably shouldn't have tried to be funny. I shouldn't have said 'Bea, you *had* one, but I wrecked it.' But that was no reason for her to get angry. She didn't have to rub it in by asking, 'Why on earth did you take my car? You haven't driven a car for years.' Of course I haven't driven a car for years. Who needs a car in Manhattan? Besides, when we do need to go by car, she always drives. And who took off for Paris in the middle of the semester anyway? She or I? So I told her, 'Bea, this is too long a story over the phone. I'll give you the details when I get home.' 'What do you mean, home?' she shot back. 'Where are you now?' When she heard that I was still in the hospital, she became civil. I went on to say that the only reason I was still in the hospital was that I'd been knocked unconscious during the accident. They wanted to be sure I had nothing more serious than a broken left arm. This is when she came up with an extraordinary question. My wife of thirty-some years asked me – three thousand miles away in the hospital – whether I got the bumper stickers. No, that's not completely true; I'm jumping ahead of my story. I always tell jokes this way – I give the punch-line away too early. She first asked whether the front or the rear of the car got demolished. When I told her that it was mostly the front and the sides, she sounded relieved. Only then did she ask whether I had retrieved the bumper stickers. At first, I thought I didn't understand correctly, but when she spelled it out: 'B U M P E R S T I C K E R S', I didn't know whether to laugh or get angry. Thank God I didn't laugh, because she really meant it. Instead I said, 'Sure, I'll get your bumper stickers,' but if I'd known what I'd let myself in for, I would have kept my mouth shut.

I am supposed to be a leading Dante scholar – 'Dantesoph' she called me when I had 'Bay-ah-tre-chayed' her once too often. (It didn't help when I pointed out that she was mixing Latin and Greek). Holder of the Lamont chair at New York University; a man to whom cars are unnecessary burdens; who believes in supporting the taxi cab industry; and there I was heading for the biggest car dump in New Jersey. When we finally got there, I went up to the office, really just a shack, and asked the character in charge how I could get something from our Toyota. 'What Toyota?' he asked. 'The place is full of 'em.' That was the first problem: Bea's car was a two-year-old Toyota – I never remember whether this makes it an '85 or '86 – dark maroon, four doors, but I couldn't recall the model name. 'When did they bring it here?' he continued as he opened some notebook. 'I guess it was sometime during the last four days,' I replied. After all, I hadn't made the arrangements, I was in the hospital. And then came problem number two: 'What's the licence number?' he asked. The licence number? How on earth would I know the licence number? I don't burden my brain with such trivia. I don't even remember my social security number. Deliberately so. I'm not using up my available synapses for bureaucratic detritus which I can look up. I told him this in simple language – I figured 'detritus' was not part of his vocabulary. The man gave me a look as if I were crazy. He slammed the notebook shut. 'Find out your licence plate number and then come back.' I should've struck him dumb with 'Charon, bite back your spleen.' But I doubt he'd read Canto III of the *Inferno*.

Instead of standing up to this car undertaker, this Cerberus of an automobile inferno, I shuffled back to the taxi, went home, and called my wife, forgetting that in Paris it was twelve thirty in the morning. 'What's your car licence number?' I asked. Actually, that isn't true. I felt too foolish to start with this question. I tried to be amusing: 'Though I may come a bit late to my turn, may it not annoy you to pause and speak a while.' I could hear her groan three thousand miles away. 'Which goddamn Canto is this?' '*Inferno* XXVII,' I replied, but she didn't think it was funny or clever, not at twelve thirty a.m. So I got to the point: if she wanted me to get her bumper stickers, I first had to find the car, and for that I had to have the licence number. And then I got another surprise. 'DO IT,' she said in a voice that had lost all drowsiness. At first I didn't understand. 'Do what?' I asked. But then she explained that this is what our licence plate said. 'What do you mean, ours? Yours!' I wanted to make it clear that in no way was I going to be associated with such a preposterous label. But how could it be possible that in two years of riding in the front passenger seat of her Toyota, I never noticed the licence plate? I guess I never looked. What an asinine thing to put on a licence plate. I wonder what she meant by DO IT? But then I had to admit that I hadn't even noticed that the car had any bumper stickers. 'Do you know what your problem is?' asked my wife. 'Long promise and short observance. *Inferno*, same Canto.' If she hadn't hung up immediately, I would have shouted '*Brava*.'

I was still puzzled over how I'd managed to overlook the licence plate. Do many people really know what's on their car licence plates? I decided to perform as random an experiment as possible: I would question the first three colleagues that I bumped into at lunch at the faculty club. As luck would have it, my first victim turned out to be a philosopher, Jerome Scheldrich. He just guffawed. 'Who owns a car in

Manhattan?' was all he said. Noel Fenton was next. He immediately admitted that he didn't know the licence plate number of his car, never had known it, and then – psychologist that he was – started to give me a detailed analysis of why he never remembered his own licence plate. I just beamed. At this point I changed the rules of my private survey: when I saw one of my own colleagues, Mario Bonomico, at a table, I decided to ask him. A good Italian, he turned out to be the most interesting and also the most sympathetic subject. He did, in fact, know his licence plate but only because of some heroic mnemonic device. He'd worked it out when his car was once towed away after he had blithely ignored a P.A. announcement about an illegally parked automobile with his licence number. Somehow, I felt that the score was still 3-0 in my favour.

The next day I took another cab to the dump. I hate to think what I spent on these cab trips. If I had to have an accident, why, I ask, didn't I have it in Manhattan? Anyway, the same character was sitting at his desk.
My God, I thought, *Inferno*, Canto V.

> 'There Minos sits, grinning, grotesque, and hale.
> He examines each lost soul as it arrives
> and delivers his verdict with his coiling tail.'

He recognized me right away. 'Well, what's the licence number?' he asked, in a pretty condescending manner. 'DO IT,' I almost shouted. 'What ya mean, do it?' exclaimed Minos. 'Do what?' I couldn't help laughing and then told him about the licence plate. I guess that broke the ice; after looking in his book, he actually took me out into his empire. All I could think of was Cantos XXVII-XXX in the *Inferno*. Just as Dante made 'the circuit of the pit', seeing 'torn bodies mangled and split open', I stared at this incredible conglomeration of automobile carcasses. The man pointed in the general direction of the left fence and then departed with the words 'your Toyota oughta be in there'. While I stumbled around looking for a maroon wreck, two tow trucks arrived, one after another, to drop their smashed-up loads near me. So I dropped Dante and focused on this Jersey car dump. I had to be careful, with my arm in a cast, climbing around the wrecks. Finally I found 'DO IT' – it was practically staring me in the face, but I was so overwhelmed by the mess that I had initially overlooked it. And there were the bumper stickers. The print was small on the first one I saw and splattered with mud. Still I could make out part of the text: 'Richest soil the soonest will grow wild …' Can you imagine, we drove around in a car saying this and I didn't even know it? There was a familiar ring about it, like a message in a Chinese fortune cookie, but what on earth was it supposed to mean on her rear bumper? I figured that I could work out the meaning when I got home. At this point all I wanted was to get out of the place with the bumper stickers. Then it struck me: I had forgotten to bring along a knife or razor blade. How was I going to detach the stickers? I went back to the shack to ask the man whether he could lend me a razor blade. 'What for?' he asked curiously. When I explained to him that I wanted to remove some bumper stickers, he first looked puzzled and then, in a remarkably kind voice, provided a startling piece of information: 'Razor blades make a mess. It's a cinch with a hairdryer.' I didn't have to tell him that I do not usually travel with hairdryers. So I told the man that I might as well take the entire rear bumper and asked whether he would remove it for me. He gave me a sly look. 'Sure, but it'll cost forty bucks.' 'Forty dollars!' I protested. 'This is *my* car.' 'This *was* your car,' he retorted. 'We get them wrecks 'cause we store 'em here. If you wanna pay storage charges ... let's see, how long was your car here?' So I paid him. It was amazing how fast he got the bumper off, but you should have seen the face of the cab driver when the two of us arrived with a filthy bumper and asked him to put it in his boot.

For once, I regretted living in a faculty apartment. I would gladly have forgotten about the subsidized rent in exchange for standard Manhattan apartment anonymity. In this place, you're not just apartment 9A, or the man in 14E. You're Jasper Ellis Duff from the Law School (why do these lawyers always spell out their middle names?) or Serge Goronsky from Math. These people know your departmental scuttlebutt before you even get home. That day was no exception. As I got into the elevator with the filthy bumper in my good arm, none other than Mrs Basamutary, the nosiest person in the entire place, stepped in. 'Professor Trippett,' she asked before the door had even closed completely, 'what are you doing with that object?' Thank God I was holding it so that the bumper stickers were facing my jacket. I just shrugged my shoulders and asked about her husband. Still, I am willing to bet that before that evening passed few people in the apartment building hadn't heard about Professor Lionel Trippett, of the

Italian Department, clutching a dirty bumper in his right arm, as his left one was in a cast.

As soon as I entered our apartment I took the 'object' into the bath tub and hosed it down. God, was it filthy! The bath tub was a mess, so I cleaned it while the bumper was drying. I then looked for a hairdryer. Of course there wasn't one. Bea had taken it to Paris. I was in no mood to go out again to buy one. I wondered where I could borrow a dryer in this apartment house without starting on a new list of questions. And then I remembered Professor Mitsuhashi, a new faculty member from Japan. His fractured English and that he was a chemist were sufficient grounds that our acquaintance had not progressed beyond the nodding stage. The Mitsuhashis turned out to be a good choice. His wife opened the door; all I got was a startled 'ah so' and the hairdryer. I wonder whether she ever told her husband about the '*Grazie, bellissima*' when I returned the dryer.

I sat down to inspect the stickers. There were three of them, all of uniform size, the print unusually small. One would have needed superb vision to read the fairly lengthy message from another car. Now, of course, I had them within arm's length and, in addition, I wore my reading glasses. But as I cautiously aimed the hairdryer on the stickers and started to peel them off, I found another set of bumper stickers underneath them, and then a third layer. They had been glued on top of each other, rather carefully I must say, so that only three showed at any one time.

Suddenly I got goose pimples all over. The word 'intellection' on one of the bumper stickers and the 3×3 theme had registered almost simultaneously. For

Dante, 3 was the ultimate number: 3 parts to his Divine Comedy; 3 lines to each stanza; 33 Cantos for each part; 3 times 3, the magic number 9, to describe his Beatrice. But I bet that few people have ever heard of 'intellection', even though it's in the dictionary. However, it does occur in a couple of English versions of Dante – John Ciardi's and Mark Musa's translations of the Divine Comedy. Not in any of the others: Cary's, Binyon's, Singleton's, Sisson's, Carlyle-Wicksteed's, Mandelbaum's or Anderson's. I know all of them – that's my business. As a student I was brought up on the real classic – Francis Cary – but Ciardi's is the most colloquial, in fact the only even faintly bumperstickerish one. My Bea! My fantastic Bay-ah-tree-chay! I was so excited I spread the nine stickers out on the rug and numbered them: 1, 2 and 3 were the original three stickers that I uncovered last from the hairdryer treatment. Numbers 7, 8 and 9, of course, were chronologically the most recent. The one that I saw at the car dump turned out to be Bea's bumper canto number 8.

THE TOYOTA CANTOS

1. Burning logs, when poked, let fly a fountain of innumerable sparks. *Par*. XVIII
   I do not hide my heart from you. *Inf*. X
2. The record may say much in little space: *Par* XIX
   Mortal imperfection ... makes fit for intellection. *Par*. IV
3. You seem to lack all knowledge of the present. *Inf*. X
   Why, when every lower sphere sounds the sweet symphony of paradise ... there is no music here. *Par*. XXI

4. Why does your understanding stray so far from its own habit? *Inf.* XI
It is no learning to understand what one does not retain. *Par.* V
5. Portion out more wisely the time allotted us. *Pur.* XXIII
If you understand me, show that you mean to profit from your time. *Inf.* XXIV
6. Lift your head. This is no time to be shut up in your own thoughts. *Pur.* XII
Look deep, look well, however your eyes may smart. *Pur.* XXXI
7. Take care. Do not let go of me. Take care. *Pur.* XVI
The taste of love grown wrathful is a bitterness. *Pur.* XXX
8. Richest soil the soonest will grow wild with bad seed and neglect. *Pur.* XXX
9. Look at me well, I am she. I am Beatrice. *Pur.* XXX
Losing me, all may perhaps be lost. *Par.* II

The time has come to make a confession: At that stage, all I had stumbled upon was the Dante numerology – admittedly a powerful key – and one word 'intellection,' which turned out to be my Rosetta stone. I pounced again on Bea's nine bumper cantos – I rather liked the term and promptly made it part of my private vocabulary – to check for other Dante attributions. Portions of bumper cantos 1, 3, 8 and 9 turned out to be quite easy – especially number 9 ending with 'I am Beatrice'. By now I was convinced that all had their Divine Comedy counterparts.

At least three hours passed, in what proved to be a devilishly delicious game, before I woke up to the fact that I was doing precisely what Bea had been criticizing through her bumper *Tragica Commedia*. Clearly the point was to understand *what* she was saying, not *where* in Dante the quote could be found. I stopped looking for hints in the bumper cantos to Dante's Cantos. Instead, I re-read them just for content and the message started to penetrate.

But let me return to my story. My new secretary's name is Jennifer. It's amazing how many young women in their middle twenties are called Jennifer these days. This Jennifer is one of the most efficient secretaries I've ever had. What's more, she's remarkably discreet. I figured she was precisely the person who could help me. 'Jennifer,' I said. I never use Jenny or any other nickname with her, and I think that she appreciates it. Where can one order specially-made bumper stickers?' This was likely to be a peculiar question for any man in his fifties, not just a professor of Italian literature. Nevertheless, Jennifer pretended as if this were the most natural question that could be presented to an academic secretary; especially one whose typing deals largely with fourteenth-century affairs. Within minutes she produced the name of a place in Soho that sold buttons, every kind of corny message, and lots of bumper stickers. She'd even confirmed by telephone that special orders could be filled within forty-eight hours.

The place was amazing. I must've browsed for a couple of hours when suddenly I found exactly what I needed. I only wished I'd thought of it myself. I still don't know why it was buried among the environmental texts: the whale preservation and no-nuke messages. I handed the slip of paper with the code number to the clerk. 'Do you have this bumper sticker in stock, or do you have to print it?' I inquired. 'Karma?' the man read. 'Oh yeah, I get it. Where did you find that one? That's a new one on me. Lemme see if we have it.' I stopped him. 'Wait,' I said, 'can you print that message for me but add a couple more words?'

I'd phoned Bea again in France that there was no reason for her to cancel her return charter flight reservation – the arm in the cast didn't hurt any more, and luckily it was the left one. This gave me plenty of time to get the new bumper sticker and to ask Jennifer for a second personal favour. I'm not someone who uses his secretary for personal errands, but in this instance Jennifer understood why I needed her help. I wanted the old bumper to be highly polished – it was to serve as my new palette – and this was difficult to do with one arm in a cast. Furthermore, I wanted it wrapped in fancy gift paper with a large bow and I've always been a lousy wrapper of presents, even without a broken arm. But I didn't tell this to Jennifer.

Before I took the taxi to Kennedy airport to pick up Bea, I placed the long package on the coffee table with the big manila envelope on top of it. It contained the new Toyota sales receipt, the nine carefully dried and chronologically arranged old bumper stickers, and a brief letter. Writing it turned out to be a lot of work – much more than I bargained for – but Bea had set a precedent. It became my version of her bumper cantos, interspersed with some original Lionel Trippett.

'Oh my Beatrice, sweet and loving guide' –
I need not tell you where this opening comes from. At one time, it probably would have been

typical of me to say that I am not 'persuaded to give ear to arguments, whose force is not made clear.' But in spite of this quote's origin (Par. XVII) *it is unlikely to lead us to Paradise.*

I could have answered: 'The only fit reply to a fit request is silence and the fact' (Inf. XXIV) *and added: 'I have no recollection of ever having been estranged from you'* (Pur XXXIII).

I could have complained: 'How sharp the sting of a small fault is to your sense' (Pur. III).

I could have equivocated: 'Or have I missed your true intent and read some other there?' (Pur. VI).

But I am sure that you – who seem to have studied Dante in a way so different from mine – would have replied 'the sense of what I wrote is plain, if you bring all your wits to bear upon it' (Pur VI). *Therefore, I have taken your advice: 'Look deep. Look well' and Dante's* (Pur. VIII): *'If you seek truth, sharpen your eyes.' Now that I understand 'often, indeed, appearances give rise to groundless doubts in us, and false conclusions, the true cause being hidden from our eyes'* (Pur. XXII), *I promise: 'I shall from now on no longer speak like one but half awake'* (Pur. XXXIII).

If I 'look closely now into that part of me ... the part with which I see' (Par. XX), *I realize that I took many things for granted. I was about to list these, but you should really hear them from my own mouth. You should question me; perhaps the way Dante was questioned before he was found to be deserving of paradise. I would like to do something that, strangely enough, we have never done in all our years of marriage: reading Dante together. Your 'bumper cantos' – this is what I named your messages that, literally and figuratively, I never saw – showed me that there is at least one more way of reading the Divine Comedy. For once, I want to see it your way, because 'the most blest condition is based on the act of seeing, not of love, love being the act that follows recognition.' As you can imagine, this comes from Paradiso and I would like our joint reading to start with Canto XXVIII.*

I cannot resist ending this letter with a line from Dante's very last Canto: 'I feel my joy swell and my spirits warm.' I hope yours will too when you open the accompanying package.

Lionel

On the way back from Kennedy airport, I purposely refrained from talking about the accident or the car. I insisted that Bea tell me about her stay in Paris. It was the first time in years that she'd gone alone to Europe, so it was only natural that I'd be curious. I started getting nervous as we got into our elevator. Thank God, there was no Mrs Basamutary, not even Mrs Mitsuhashi, in the elevator. I led her straight into the living-room and waited until she saw the package and envelope. 'What's this?' she asked. 'It's for you,' I replied, 'but first open the envelope.' Bea gave me a curious look and then tore open the large, brown envelope. The sight of the old familiar bumper stickers produced a nervous laugh, which stopped as she started to read my letter. 'Oh Lionel,' she said in a totally unfamiliar tone, 'you don't really have to ...' 'It's OK,' I said. 'Just open the package.'

Carefully she opened the package, so as not to tear the wrapping paper. She was a compulsive saver of ribbons and paper – it drove me berserk at times to see her unwrap birthday presents. But this time, I didn't mind. I wanted everything to happen in slow motion.

'Oh Lionel! Lionel, you nut, you didn't have to,'

she murmured. 'You're repeating yourself, dear,' I said and that's when she started to cry. She hadn't done so for years. Strange. After all, the only thing the new sticker said was 'Your Karma Finally Drove Over My Dogma. (Lionel, *Purgatorio*, Canto Unico).'